MW01714162

CHRISTIANA'S JOURNEY

Part 2 of The Pilgrim's Progress

JOHN BUNYAN

LUMEN

CHRISTIAN PRODUCTS

LUMEN Christian Products®
Elizabethton, Tennessee

Cover and interior design: Dickinson Press
ISBN: 978-1-939900-10-4

LUMEN Christian Products
is a division of Send The Light Distribution
"Our Name is Our Mission"

Printed in the United States of America

John Bunyan

John Bunyan was a popular preacher as well as a prolific author. This portrait was drawn by his friend, Robert White. Bunyan was tall, had reddish hair, a prominent nose, a rather large mouth, and sparkling eyes. Rudyard Kipling once referred to him as "the father of the novel." Bunyan wrote *The Pilgrim's Progress* from his jail cell, where he was imprisoned for preaching without a license. During his incarceration, he wove shoelaces to support his family and preached to his fellow prisoners—a congregation of about sixty. In his possession were two books, Foxe's Book of Martyrs, and the Bible, a violin he had made out of tin, a flute he'd made from a chair leg and a supply of pen and paper. Both music and writing were integral to John Bunyan's life.

CONTENTS

I have used similtudes.--Hos. 12:10

THE AUTHOR'S WAY OF SENDING FORTH HIS SECOND PART OF THE PILGRIM

Go, now, my little Book, to every place
Where my first Pilgrim has but shown his face:
Call at their door: if any say, Who's there?
Then answer thou, Christiana is here.
If they bid thee come in, then enter thou,
With all thy boys; and then, as thou know'st how,
Tell who they are, also from whence they came;
Perhaps they'll know them by their looks, or name:
But if they should not, ask them yet again,
If formerly they did not entertain
One Christian, a Pilgrim? If they say
They did, and were delighted in his way;
Then let them know that these related were
Unto him; yea, his wife and children are.

Tell them, that they have left their house and home;
Are turned Pilgrims; seek a world to come;
That they have met with hardships in the way;
That they do meet with troubles night and day;

That they have trod on serpents; fought with devils;
Have also overcome a many evils;
Yea, tell them also of the next who have,
Of love to pilgrimage, been stout and brave
Defenders of that way; and how they still
Refuse this world to do their Father's will.
Go tell them also of those dainty things
That pilgrimage unto the Pilgrim brings.
Let them acquainted be, too, how they are
Beloved of their King, under his care;
What goodly mansions he for them provides;
Though they meet with rough winds and swelling tides,
How brave a calm they will enjoy at last,
Who to their Lord, and by his ways hold fast.

Perhaps with heart and hand they will embrace
Thee, as they did my firstling; and will grace
Thee and thy fellows with such cheer and fare,
As show well, they of Pilgrims lovers are.

The First Objection:
But how if they will not believe of me
That I am truly thine? cause some there be
That counterfeit the Pilgrim and his name,
Seek, by disguise, to seem the very same;
And by that means have wrought themselves into
The hands and houses of I know not who.

Answer:
'Tis true, some have, of late, to counterfeit
My Pilgrim, to their own my title set;
Yea, others half my name, and title too,
Have stitched to their books, to make them do.
But yet they, by their features, do declare
Themselves not mine to be, whose'er they are.

If such thou meet'st with, then thine only way
Before them all, is, to say out thy say
In thine own native language, which no man
Now useth, nor with ease dissemble can.

If, after all, they still of you shall doubt,
Thinking that you, like gypsies, go about,
In naughty wise the country to defile;
Or that you seek good people to beguile
With things unwarrantable; send for me,
And I will testify you pilgrims be;
Yea, I will testify that only you
My Pilgrims are, and that alone will do.

The Second Objection:
But yet, perhaps, I may enquire for him
Of those who wish him damned life and limb.
What shall I do, when I at such a door
For Pilgrims ask, and they shall rage the more?

Answer:
Fright not thyself, my Book, for such bugbears
Are nothing else but groundless fears.
My Pilgrim's book has traveled sea and land,
Yet could I never come to understand
That it was slighted or turned out of door
By any Kingdom, were they rich or poor.
In France and Flanders, where men kill each other,
My Pilgrim is esteemed a friend, a brother.

In Holland, too, 'tis said, as I am told,
My Pilgrim is with some, worth more than gold.
Highlanders and wild Irish can agree
My Pilgrim should familiar with them be.

'Tis in New England under such advance,
Receives there so much loving countenance,
As to be trimm'd, newcloth'd, and deck'd with gems,
That it might show its features, and its limbs.
Yet more: so comely doth my Pilgrim walk,
That of him thousands daily sing and talk.

If you draw nearer home, it will appear
My Pilgrim knows no ground of shame or fear:
City and country will him entertain,
With Welcome, Pilgrim; yea, they can't refrain
From smiling, if my Pilgrim be but by,
Or shows his head in any company.

Brave gallants do my Pilgrim hug and love,
Esteem it much, yea, value it above
Things of greater bulk; yea, with delight
Say, my lark's leg is better than a kite.
Young ladies, and young gentlewomen too,
Do not small kindness to my Pilgrim show;
Their cabinets, their bosoms, and their hearts,
My Pilgrim has; 'cause he to them imparts
His pretty riddles in such wholesome strains,
As yield them profit double to their pains
Of reading; yea, I think I may be bold
To say some prize him far above their gold.
The very children that do walk the street,
If they do but my holy Pilgrim meet,
Salute him will; will wish him well, and say,
He is the only stripling of the day.

They that have never seen him, yet admire
What they have heard of him, and much desire
To have his company, and hear him tell
Those Pilgrim stories which he knows so well.

Yea, some that did not love him at first,
But called him fool and noddy, say they must,
Now they have seen and heard him, him commend
And to those whom they love they do him send.

Wherefore, my Second Part, thou need'st not be

Afraid to show thy head: none can hurt thee,
That wish but well to him that went before;
'Cause thou com'st after with a second store
Of things as good, as rich, as profitable,
For young, for old, for stagg'ring, and for stable.

The Third Objection:
But some there be that say, He laughs too loud
And some do say, His Head is in a cloud.
Some say, His words and stories are so dark,
They know not how, by them, to find his mark.

Answer:
One may, I think, say, Both his laughs and cries
May well be guessed at by his wat'ry eyes.
Some things are of that nature, as to make
One's fancy chuckle, while his heart doth ache:
When Jacob saw his Rachel with the sheep,
He did at the same time both kiss and weep.

Whereas some say, A cloud is in his head;
That doth but show his wisdom's covered
With its own mantles--and to stir the mind
To search well after what it fain would find,
Things that seem to be hid in words obscure
Do but the godly mind the more allure
To study what those sayings should contain,
That speak to us in such a cloudy strain.

I also know a dark similitude
Will on the curious fancy more intrude,
And will stick faster in the heart and head,
Than things from similes not borrowed.

Wherefore, my Book, let no discouragement
Hinder thy travels. Behold, thou art sent
To friends, not foes; to friends that will give place
To thee, thy pilgrims, and thy words embrace.

Besides, what my first Pilgrim left concealed,
Thou, my brave second Pilgrim, hast revealed;
What Christian left lock'd up, and went his way,
Sweet Christiana opens with her key.

The Fourth Objection:
But some love not the method of your first:
Romance they count it; throw't away as dust.
If I should meet with such, what should I say?
Must I slight them as they slight me, or nay?

Answer:
My Christiana, if with such thou meet,
By all means, in all loving wise them greet;
Render them not reviling for revile,
But, if they frown, I prithee on them smile:
Perhaps 'tis nature, or some ill report,
Has made them thus despise, or thus retort.

Some love no fish, some love no cheese, and some
Love not their friends, nor their own house or home;
Some start at pig, slight chicken, love not fowl
More than they love a cuckoo or an owl.
Leave such, my Christiana, to their choice,
And seek those who to find thee will rejoice;
By no means strive, but, in most humble wise,
Present thee to them in thy Pilgrim's guise.

Go then, my little Book, and show to all
That entertain and bid thee welcome shall,
What thou shalt keep close shut up from the rest;
And wish what thou shalt show them may be bless'd
To them for good, and make them choose to be
Pilgrims, by better far than thee or me.
Go, then, I say, tell all men who thou art:
Say, I am Christiana; and my part
Is now, with my four sons, to tell you what
It is for men to take a Pilgrim's lot.

Go, also, tell them who and what they be
That now do go on pilgrimage with thee;
Say, Here's my neighbor Mercy: she is one
That has long time with me a pilgrim gone:
Come, see her in her virgin face, and learn
'Twixt idle ones and pilgrims to discern.
Yea, let young damsels learn of her to prize
The world which is to come, in any wise.

When little tripping maidens follow God,
And leave old doting sinners to his rod,
'Tis like those days wherein the young ones cried
Hosanna! when the old ones did deride.

Next tell them of old Honest, whom you found
With his white hairs treading the Pilgrim's ground;
Yea, tell them how plain-hearted this man was;
How after his good Lord he bare the cross.
Perhaps with some gray head, this may prevail
With Christ to fall in love, and sin bewail.

Tell them also, how Master Fearing went
On pilgrimage, and how the time he spent
In solitariness, with fears and cries;
And how, at last, he won the joyful prize.
He was a good man, though much down in spirit;
He is a good man, and doth life inherit.

Tell them of Master Feeble-mind also,
Who not before, but still behind would go.
Show them also, how he had like been slain,
And how one Great-Heart did his life regain.
This man was true of heart; though weak in grace,
One might true godliness read in his face.

Then tell them of Master Ready-to-Halt,
A man with crutches, but much without fault.

Tell them how Master Feeble-mind and he
Did love, and in opinion much agree.
And let all know, though weakness was their chance,
Yet sometimes one could sing, the other dance.

Forget not Master Valiant-for-the-Truth,
That man of courage, though a very youth:
Tell everyone his spirit was so stout,
No man could ever make him face about;
And how Great-Heart and he could not forbear,
But pull down Doubting-Castle, slay Despair!

Overlook not Master Despondency,
Nor Much-afraid, his daughter, though they lie
Under such mantles, as may make them look
(With some) as if their God had them forsook.
They softly went, but sure; and, at the end,
Found that the Lord of Pilgrims was their friend.
When thou hast told the world of all these things,
Then turn about, my Book, and touch these strings;
Which, if but touched, will such music make,
They'll make a cripple dance, a giant quake.

Those riddles that lie couched within thy breast,
Freely propound, expound; and for the rest
Of thy mysterious lines, let them remain
For those whose nimble fancies shall them gain.

Now may this little Book a blessing be
To those who love this little Book and me;
And may its buyer have no cause to say,
His money is but lost or thrown away.
Yea, may this second Pilgrim yield that fruit
As may with each good Pilgrim's fancy suit;
And may it some persuade, that go astray,
To turn their feet and heart to the right way,

Is the hearty prayer of
The Author,
JOHN BUNYAN

TO THE READER

Courteous companions:

Some time since, to tell you my dream that I had of Christian the pilgrim, and of his dangerous journey towards the Celestial country, was pleasant to me and profitable to you. I told you then also what I saw concerning his wife and children, and how unwilling they were to go with him on pilgrimage; insomuch that he was forced to go on his progress without them; for he durst not run the danger of that destruction which he feared would come by staying with them in the City of Destruction: wherefore, as I then showed you, he left them and departed.

Now it hath so happened, through the multiplicity of business, that I have been much hindered and kept back from my wonted travels into those parts whence he went, and so could not, till now, obtain an opportunity to make further inquiry after those whom he left behind, that I might give you an account of them. But having had some concerns that way of late, I went down again thitherward. Now, having taken up my lodging in a wood about a mile off the place, as I slept, I dreamed again.

And as I was in my dream, behold, an aged gentleman came by where I lay; and, because he was to go some part of the way that I was traveling, methought I got up and went with him. So, as we walked, and as travelers usually do, I was as if we fell into a discourse; and our talk happened to be about Christian and his travels; for thus I began with the old man:

Sir, said I, what town is that there below, that lieth on the left hand of our way?

Then said Mr. Sagacity, (for that was his name,) It is the City of Destruction, a populous place, but possessed with a very ill-conditioned and idle sort of people.

I thought that was that city, quoth I; I went once myself through that town; and therefore know that this report you give of it is true.

Mr. Sagacity: Too true! I wish I could speak truth in speaking better of them that dwell therein.

Well, sir, quoth I, then I perceive you to be a well-meaning man, and so one that takes pleasure to hear and tell of that which is good. Pray, did you never hear what happened to a man some time ago of this town, (whose name was Christian,) that went on a pilgrimage up towards the higher regions?

Mr. Sagacity: Hear of him! Aye, and I also heard of the molestations, troubles, wars, captivities, cries, groans, frights, and fears, that he met with and had on his journey. Besides, I must tell you, all our country rings of him; there are but few houses that have heard of him and his doings, but have sought after and got the records of his pilgrimage; yea, I think I may say that his hazardous journey has got many well-wishers to his ways; for, though when he was here he was fool in every man's mouth, yet now he is gone he is highly commended of all. For 'tis said he lives bravely where he is: yea, many of them that are resolved never to run his hazards, yet have their mouths water at his gains.

They may, quoth I, well think, if they think anything that is true, that he liveth well where he is; for he now lives at, and in the fountain of life, and has what he has without labor and sorrow, for there is no grief mixed therewith. But, pray what talk have the people about him?

Mr. Sagacity: Talk! the people talk strangely about him: some say that he now walks in white, (Rev. 3:4); that he has a chain of gold about his neck; that he has a crown of gold, beset with pearls, upon his head: others say, that the shining ones, who sometimes showed themselves to him in his journey, are become his companions, and that he is as familiar with them where he is, as here one neighbor is with another. Besides, it is confidently affirmed concerning him, that the King of the place where he is has bestowed upon him already a very rich and pleasant dwelling at court, and that he every day eateth and drinketh, and walketh and talketh with him, and receiveth of the smiles and favors of him that is Judge of all there. (Zech. 3:7; Luke 14:14,15). Moreover, it is expected of some, that his Prince, the Lord of that country, will shortly come into these parts, and will know the reason, if they can give any, why his neighbors set so little by him, and had him so much in derision, when they perceived that he would be a pilgrim. (Jude, 14,15).

For they say, that now he is so in the affections of his Prince, that his Sovereign is so much concerned with the indignities that were cast upon Christian when he became a pilgrim, that he will look upon all as if done unto himself, (Luke 10:16); and no marvel, for it was for the love that he had to his Prince that he ventured as he did.

I dare say, quoth I; I am glad on't; I am glad for the poor man's sake, for that now he has rest from his labor, and for that he now reapeth the benefit of his tears with joy; and for that he has got beyond the gun-shot of his enemies, and is out of the reach of them that hate him. (Rev. 14:13; Psa. 126:5, 6). I also am glad for that a rumor of these things is noised abroad in this country; who can tell but that it may work some good effect on some that are left behind? But pray, sir, while it is fresh in my mind, do you hear anything of his wife and children? Poor hearts! I wonder in my mind what they do.

Mr. Sagacity: Who? Christiana and her sons? They are like to do as well as Christian did himself; for though they all played the fool at first, and would by no means be persuaded by either the tears or entreaties of Christian, yet second thoughts have wrought wonderfully with them: so they have packed up, and are also gone after him.

Better and better, quoth I: but, what! wife and children, and all?

Mr. Sagacity: It is true: I can give you an account of the matter, for I was upon the spot at the instant, and was thoroughly acquainted with the whole affair.

Then, said I, a man, it seems, may report it for a truth.

Mr. Sagacity: You need not fear to affirm it: I mean, that they are all gone on pilgrimage, both the good woman and her four boys. And being we are, as I perceive, going some considerable way together, I will give you an account of the whole matter.

This Christiana, (for that was her name from the day that she with her children betook themselves to a pilgrim's life,) after her husband was gone over the river, and she could hear of him no more, her thoughts began to work in her mind. First, for that she had lost her husband, and for that the loving bond of that relation was utterly broken betwixt them. For you know, said he to me, nature can do no less but entertain the living with many a heavy cogitation, in the remembrance of the loss of loving relations. This, therefore, of her husband did cost her many a tear. But this was not all; for Christiana did also begin to consider with herself, whether her unbecoming behavior towards her husband was not one cause that she saw him no more, and that in such sort he was taken away from her. And upon this came into her mind, by swarms, all her unkind, unnatural, and ungodly carriage to her dear friend; which also clogged her conscience, and did load her with guilt. She was, moreover, much broken with recalling to remembrance the restless groans, brinish tears, and self-bemoanings of her husband, and how she did harden her heart against all his entreaties and loving persuasions of her and her sons to go with him; yea, there was not anything that Christian either said to her, or did before her, all the while that his burden did hang on his back, but it returned upon her like a flash of lightning, and rent the caul of her heart in sunder; especially that bitter outcry of his, "What shall I do to be saved?" did ring in her ears most dolefully.

Then said she to her children, Sons, we are all undone. I have sinned away your father, and he is gone: he would have had us with him, but I would not go myself: I also have hindered you of life. With that the boys fell into tears, and cried out to go after their father. Oh, said Christiana, that it had been but our lot to go with him! then had it fared well with us, beyond what it is like to do now. For, though I formerly foolishly imagined, concerning the troubles of your father, that they proceeded of a foolish fancy that he had, or for that he was overrun with melancholy humors; yet now it will not out of my mind, but that they sprang from another cause; to wit, for that the light of life was given him, (James 1:23-25; John 8:12); by the help of which, as I perceive, he has escaped the snares of death. (Prov. 14:27). Then they all wept again, and cried out, Oh, woe worth the day!

The next night Christiana had a dream; and, behold, she saw as if a broad parchment was opened before her, in which were recorded the sum of her ways; and the crimes, as she thought looked very black upon her. Then she cried out aloud in her sleep, "Lord, have mercy upon me a sinner!" (Luke 18:13); and the little children heard her.

After this she thought she saw two very ill-favored ones standing by her bedside, and saying, What shall we do with this woman? for she cries out for mercy, waking and sleeping: if she be suffered to go on as she begins, we shall lose her as we have lost her husband. Wherefore we must, by one way or other, seek to take her off from the thoughts of what shall be hereafter, else all the world cannot help but she will become a pilgrim.

Now she awoke in a great sweat, also a trembling was upon her: but after a while she fell to sleeping again. And then she thought she saw Christian, her husband, in a place of bliss among many immortals, with a harp in his hand, standing and playing upon it before One that sat on a throne with a rainbow about his head. She saw also, as if he bowed his head with his face to the paved work that was under his Prince's feet, saying, "I heartily thank my Lord and King for bringing me into this place." Then shouted a company of them that stood round about, and harped with their harps; but no man living could tell what they said but Christian and his companions.

Next morning, when she was up, had prayed to God, and talked with her children a while, one knocked hard at the door; to whom she spake out, saying, "If thou comest in God's name, come in." So he said, "Amen;" and opened the door, and saluted her with, "Peace be to this house." The which when he had done, he said,

"Christiana, knowest thou wherefore I am come?" Then she blushed and trembled; also her heart began to wax warm with desires to know from whence he came, and what was his errand to her. So he said unto her, "My name is Secret; I dwell with those that are on high. It is talked of where I dwell as if thou hadst a desire to go thither: also there is a report that thou art aware of the evil thou hast formerly done to thy husband, in hardening of thy heart against his way, and in keeping of these babes in their ignorance. Christiana, the Merciful One has sent me to tell thee, that he is a God ready to forgive, and that he taketh delight to multiply the pardon of offences. He also would have thee to know, that he inviteth thee to come into his presence, to his table, and that he will feed thee with the fat of his house, and with the heritage of Jacob thy father.

"There is Christian, thy husband that was, with legions more, his companions, ever beholding that face that doth minister life to beholders; and they will all be glad when they shall hear the sound of thy feet step over thy Father's threshold."

Christiana at this was greatly abashed in herself, and bowed her head to the ground. This visitor proceeded, and said, "Christiana, here is also a letter for thee, which I have brought from thy husband's King." So she took it, and opened it, but it smelt after the manner of the best perfume. (Song 1:3). Also it was written in letters of gold. The contents of the letter were these, That the King would have her to do as did Christian her husband; for that was the way to come to his city, and to dwell in his presence with joy forever. At this the good woman was quite overcome; so she cried out to her visitor, Sir, will you carry me and my children with you, that we also may go and worship the King?

Then said the visitor, Christiana, the bitter is before the sweet. Thou must through troubles, as did he that went before thee, enter this Celestial City. Wherefore I advise thee to do as did Christian thy husband: go to the Wicket-gate yonder, over the plain, for that stands at the head of the way up which thou must go; and I wish thee all good speed. Also I advise that thou put this letter in thy bosom, that thou read therein to thyself and to thy children until you have got it by heart; for it is one of the songs that thou must sing while thou art in this house of thy pilgrimage, (Psalm 119:54); also this thou must deliver in at the further gate.

Now I saw in my dream, that this old gentleman, as he told me the story, did himself seem to be greatly affected therewith. He moreover proceeded, and said, So Christiana called her sons together, and began thus to address herself unto them: "My sons, I have, as you may perceive, been of late under much exercise in my soul about the death of your father: not for that I doubt at all of his happiness, for I am satisfied now that he is well. I have also been much affected with the thoughts of my own state and yours, which I verily believe is by nature miserable. My carriage also to your father in his distress is a great load to my conscience; for I hardened both mine own heart and yours against him, and refused to go with him on pilgrimage.

The thoughts of these things would now kill me outright, but that for a dream which I had last night, and but that for the encouragement which this stranger has given me this morning. Come, my children, let us pack up, and begone to the gate that leads to the Celestial country, that we may see your father, and be with him and his companions in peace, according to the laws of that land.

Then did her children burst out into tears, for joy that the heart of their mother was so inclined. So their visitor bid them farewell; and they began to prepare to set out for their journey.

But while they were thus about to be gone, two of the women that were Christiana's neighbors came up to her house, and knocked at her door. To whom she said as before, If you come in God's name, come in. At this the women were stunned; for this kind of language they used not to hear, or to perceive to drop from the lips of Christiana. Yet they came in: but behold, they found the good woman preparing to be gone from her house.

So they began, and said, Neighbor, pray what is your meaning by this?

Christiana answered, and said to the eldest of them, whose name was Mrs. Timorous, I am preparing for a journey.

This Timorous was daughter to him that met Christian upon the Hill of Difficulty, and would have had him go back for fear of the lions.

Timorous: For what journey, I pray you?

Christiana: Even to go after my good husband. And with that she fell a weeping.

Timorous: I hope not so, good neighbor; pray, for your poor children's sake, do not so unwomanly cast away yourself.

Christiana: Nay, my children shall go with me; not one of them is willing to stay behind.

Timorous: I wonder in my very heart what or who has brought you into this mind!

Christiana: O neighbor, knew you but as much as I do, I doubt not but that you would go along with me.

Timorous: Prithee, what new knowledge hast thou got, that so worketh off thy mind from thy friends, and that tempteth thee to go nobody knows where?

Christiana: Then Christiana replied, I have been sorely afflicted since my husband's departure from me; but especially since he went over the river. But that which troubleth me most is, my churlish carriage to him when he was under his distress. Besides, I am now as he was then; nothing will serve me but going on pilgrimage. I was a dreaming last night that I saw him. O that my soul was with him! He dwelleth in the presence of the King of the country; he sits and eats with him at his table; he is become a companion of immortals, and has a house now given him to dwell in, to which the best palace on earth, if compared, seems to me but a dunghill. (2 Cor. 5:1-4). The Prince of the place has also sent for me, with promise of entertainment, if I shall come to him; his messenger was here even now, and has brought me a letter, which invites me to come. And with that she plucked out her letter, and read it, and said to them, What now will you say to this?

Timorous: Oh, the madness that has possessed thee and thy husband, to run yourselves upon such difficulties! You have heard, I am sure what your husband did meet with, even in a manner at the first step that he took on his way, as our neighbor Obstinate can yet testify, for he went along with him; yea, and Pliable too, until they, like wise men, were afraid to go any further. We also heard, over and above, how he met with the lions, Apollyon, the Shadow of Death, and many other things. Nor is the danger that he met with at Vanity Fair to be forgotten by thee. For if he, though a man, was so hard put to it, what canst thou, being but a poor woman, do? Consider also, that these four sweet babes are thy children, thy flesh and thy bones. Wherefore, though thou shouldest be so rash as to cast away thyself, yet, for the sake of the fruit of thy body, keep thou at home.

But Christiana said unto her, Tempt me not, my neighbor: I have now a price put into my hands to get gain, and I should be a fool of the greatest size if I should have no heart to strike in with the opportunity. And for that you tell me of all these troubles which I am like to meet with in the way, they are so far from being to me a discouragement, that they show I am in the right. The bitter must come before the sweet, and that also will make the sweet the sweeter. Wherefore, since you came not to my house in God's name, as I said, I pray you to be gone, and not to disquiet me further.

Then Timorous reviled her, and said to her fellow, Come, neighbor Mercy, let us leave her in her own hands, since she scorns our counsel and company. But Mercy was at a stand, and could not so readily comply with her neighbor; and that for a twofold reason.

1. Her bowels yearned over Christiana. So she said within herself, if my neighbor will needs be gone, I will go a little way with her, and help her.

2. Her bowels yearned over her own soul; for what Christiana had said had taken some hold upon her mind.

Wherefore she said within herself again, I will yet have more talk with this Christiana; and, if I find truth and life in what she shall say, I myself with my heart shall also go with her. Wherefore Mercy began thus to reply to her neighbor Timorous:

Mercy: Neighbor, I did indeed come with you to see Christiana this morning; and since she is, as you see, taking of her last farewell of the country, I think to walk this sunshiny morning a little with her, to help her on her way. But she told her not of her second reason, but kept it to herself.

Timorous: Well, I see you have a mind to go a fooling too; but take heed in time, and be wise: while we are out of danger, we are out; but when we are in, we are in.

So Mrs. Timorous returned to her house, and Christiana betook herself to her journey. But when Timorous was got home to her house she sends for some of her neighbors, to wit, Mrs. Bat's-Eyes, Mrs. Inconsiderate, Mrs. Light-Mind, and Mrs. Know-Nothing. So when they were come to her house, she falls to telling of the story of Christiana, and of her intended journey. And thus she began her tale:

Timorous: Neighbors, having had little to do this morning, I went to give Christiana a visit; and when I came at the door I knocked, as you know it is our custom; and she answered, If you come in God's name, come in. So in I went, thinking all was well; but, when I came in I found her preparing herself to depart the town, she, and also her children. So I asked her what was her meaning by that. And she told me, in short, that she was now of a mind to go on pilgrimage, as did her husband. She told me also of a dream that she had, and how the King of the country where her husband was, had sent an inviting letter to come thither.

Then said Mrs. Know-Nothing, And what, do you think she will go?

Timorous: Aye, go she will, whatever comes on't; and methinks I know it by this; for that which was my great argument to persuade her to stay at home, (to wit, the troubles she was like to meet with on the way,) is one great argument with her to put her forward on her journey. For she told me in so many words, The bitter goes before the sweet; yea, and forasmuch as it doth, it makes the sweet the sweeter.

Mrs. Bat's-Eyes: Oh, this blind and foolish woman! said she; and will she not take warning by her husband's afflictions? For my part, I see, if he were here again, he would rest himself content in a whole skin, and never run so many hazards for nothing.

Mrs. Inconsiderate also replied, saying, Away with such fantastical fools from the town: a good riddance, for my part, I say, of her; should she stay where she dwells, and retain this her mind, who could live quietly by her? for she will either be dumpish, or unneighborly, or talk of such matters as no wise body can abide. Wherefore, for my part, I shall never be sorry for her departure; let her go, and let better come in her room: it was never a good world since these whimsical fools dwelt in it.

Then Mrs. Light-Mind added as followeth: Come, put this kind of talk away. I was yesterday at Madam Wanton's, where we were as merry as the maids. For who do you think should be there but I and Mrs. Love-the-Flesh, and three or four more, with Mrs. Lechery, Mrs. Filth, and some others: so there we had music and dancing, and what else was meet to fill up the pleasure. And I dare say, my lady herself is an admirable well-bred gentlewoman, and Mr. Lechery is as pretty a fellow.

THE FIRST STAGE

By this time Christiana was got on her way, and Mercy went along with her: so as they went, her children being there also, Christiana began to discourse. And, Mercy, said Christiana, I take this as an unexpected favor, that thou shouldest set forth out of doors with me to accompany me a little in the way.

Mercy: Then said young Mercy, (for she was but young,) If I thought it would be to purpose to go with you, I would never go near the town any more.

Christiana: Well, Mercy, said Christiana, cast in thy lot with me: I well know what will be the end of our pilgrimage: my husband is where he would not but be for all the gold in the Spanish mines. Nor shalt thou be rejected, though thou goest but upon my invitation. The King, who hath sent for me and my children, is one that delighteth in mercy. Besides, if thou wilt, I will hire thee, and thou shalt go along with me as my servant. Yet we will have all things in common betwixt thee and me: only go along with me.

Mercy: But how shall I be ascertained that I also should be entertained? Had I this hope but from one that can tell, I would make no stick at all, but would go, being helped by Him that can help, though the way was never so tedious.

Christiana: Well, loving Mercy, I will tell thee what thou shalt do: go with me to the Wicket-gate, and there I will further inquire for thee; and if there thou shalt not meet with encouragement, I will be content that thou return to thy place: I will also pay thee for thy kindness which thou showest to me and my children, in the accompanying of us in the way that thou dost.

Mercy: Then will I go thither, and will take what shall follow; and the Lord grant that my lot may there fall, even as the King of heaven shall have his heart upon me.

Christiana then was glad at heart, not only that she had a companion, but also for that she had prevailed with this poor maid to fall in love with her own salvation. So they went on together, and Mercy began to weep. Then said Christiana, Wherefore weepeth my sister so?

Mercy: Alas! said she, who can but lament, that shall but rightly consider what a state and condition my poor relations are in, that yet remain in our sinful town? And that which makes my grief the more heavy is, because they have no instructor, nor any to tell them what is to come.

Christiana: Pity becomes pilgrims; and thou dost weep for thy friends, as my good Christian did for me when he left me: he mourned for that I would not heed nor regard him; but his Lord and ours did gather up his tears, and put them into his bottle; and now both I and thou, and these my sweet babes, are reaping the fruit and benefit of them. I hope, Mercy, that these tears of thine will not be lost; for the truth hath said, that "they that sow in tears shall reap in joy." And "he that goeth forth and weepeth, bearing precious seed, shall doubtless come again with rejoicing, bringing his sheaves with him." (Psa. 126:5, 6).

Then said Mercy,

"Let the Most Blessed be my guide,
If it be his blessed will,
Unto his gate, into his fold,
Up to his holy hill.

And let him never suffer me
To swerve, or turn aside
From his free-grace and holy ways,
Whate'er shall me betide.

And let him gather them of mine
That I have left behind;
Lord, make them pray they may be thine,
With all their heart and mind."

Now my old friend proceeded, and said, But when Christiana came to the Slough of Despond, she began to be at a stand; For, said she, this is the place in which my dear husband had like to have been smothered with mud. She perceived, also, that notwithstanding the command of the King to make this place for pilgrims good, yet it was rather worse than formerly. So I asked if that was true. Yes, said the old gentleman, too true; for many there be that pretend to be the King's laborers, and that say they are for mending the King's highways, who bring dirt and dung instead of stones, and so mar instead of mending. Here Christiana therefore, with her boys, did make a stand. But said Mercy, Come, let us venture; only let us be wary. Then they looked well to their steps, and made a shift to get staggering over.

Yet Christiana had like to have been in, and that not once or twice. Now they had no sooner got over, but they thought they heard words that said unto them, "Blessed is she that believeth; for there shall be a performance of those things which were told her from the Lord." (Luke 1:45).

Then they went on again; and said Mercy to Christiana, had I as good ground to hope for a loving reception at the Wicket-gate as you, I think no Slough of Despond would discourage me.

Well, said the other, you know your sore, and I know mine; and, good friend, we shall all have enough evil before we come to our journey's end. For can it be imagined that the people who design to attain such excellent glories as we do, and who are so envied that happiness as we are, but that we shall meet with what fears and snares, with what troubles and afflictions they can possibly assault us with that hate us?

And now Mr. Sagacity left me to dream out my dream by myself. Wherefore, methought I saw Christiana, and Mercy, and the boys, go all of them up to the gate: to which, when they were come, they betook themselves to a short debate about how they must manage their calling at the gate, and what should be said unto him that did open to them: so it was concluded, since Christiana was the eldest, that she should knock for entrance, and that she should speak to him that did open, for the rest. So Christiana began to knock, and as her poor husband did, she knocked and knocked again. But instead of any that answered, they all thought they heard as if a dog came barking upon them; a dog, and a great one too; and this made the women and children afraid. Nor durst they for a while to knock any more, for fear the mastiff should fly upon them. Now, therefore, they were greatly tumbled up and down in their minds, and knew not what to do: knock they durst not, for fear of the dog; go back they durst not, for fear the keeper of that gate should espy them as they so went, and should be offended with them; at last they thought of knocking again, and knocked more vehemently than they did at first. Then said the keeper of the gate, Who is there? So the dog left off to bark, and he opened unto them.

Then Christiana made low obeisance, and said, Let not our Lord be offended with his handmaidens, for that we have knocked at his princely gate. Then said the keeper, Whence come ye? And what is it that you would have?

Christiana answered, We are come from whence Christian did come, and upon the same errand as he; to wit, to be, if it shall please you, graciously admitted by this gate into the way that leads unto the Celestial City. And I answer, my Lord, in the next place, that I am Christiana, once the wife of Christian, that now is gotten above.

With that the keeper of the gate did marvel, saying, What, is she now become a pilgrim that but a while ago abhorred that life? Then she bowed her head, and said, Yea; and so are these my sweet babes also.

Then he took her by the hand and led her in, and said also, Suffer little children to come unto me; and with that he shut up the gate. This done, he called to a trumpeter that was above, over the gate, to entertain Christiana with shouting, and the sound of trumpet for joy. So he obeyed, and sounded, and filled the air with his melodious notes.

Now all this while poor Mercy did stand without, trembling and crying, for fear that she was rejected. But when Christiana had got admittance for herself and her boys, then she began to make intercession for Mercy.

Christiana: And she said, My Lord, I have a companion that stands yet without, that is come hither upon the same account as myself: one that is much dejected in her mind, for that she comes, as she thinks, without sending for; whereas I was sent for by my husband's King to come.

Now Mercy began to be very impatient, and each minute was as long to her as an hour; wherefore she prevented Christiana from a fuller interceding for her, by knocking at the gate herself. And she knocked then so loud that she made Christiana to start. Then said the keeper of the gate, Who is there? And Christiana said, It is my friend.

So he opened the gate, and looked out, but Mercy was fallen down without in a swoon, for she fainted, and was afraid that no gate should be opened to her.

Then he took her by the hand, and said, Damsel, I bid thee arise.

Oh, sir, said she, I am faint; there is scarce life left in me. But he answered, that one once said, "When my soul fainted within me I remembered the Lord: and my prayer came unto thee, into thy holy temple." (Jonah 2:7). Fear not, but stand upon thy feet, and tell me wherefore thou art come.

Mercy: I am come for that unto which I was never invited, as my friend Christiana was. Hers was from the King, and mine was but from her. Wherefore I fear I presume.

Keep: Did she desire thee to come with her to this place?

Mercy: Yes; and, as my Lord sees, I am come. And if there is any grace and forgiveness of sins to spare, I beseech that thy poor handmaid may be a partaker thereof.

Then he took her again by the hand, and led her gently in, and said, I pray for all them that believe on me, by what means soever they come unto me. Then said he to those that stood by, Fetch something and give it to Mercy to smell on, thereby to stay her faintings; so they fetched her a bundle of myrrh, and a while after she was revived.

And now were Christiana and her boys, and Mercy, received of the Lord at the head of the way, and spoken kindly unto by him. Then said they yet further unto him, We are sorry for our sins, and beg of our Lord his pardon, and further information what we must do.

I grant pardon, said he, by word and deed; by word in the promise of forgiveness, by deed in the way I obtained it. Take the first from my lips with a kiss, and the other as it shall be revealed. (Song 1:2; John 20:20).

Now I saw in my dream, that he spake many good words unto them, whereby they were greatly gladdened. He also had them up to the top of the gate, and showed them by what deed they were saved; and told them withal, that that sight they would have again as they went along in the way, to their comfort.

So he left them awhile in a summer parlor below, where they entered into talk by themselves; and thus Christiana began. O how glad am I that we are not in hither.

Mercy: So you well may; but I, of all, have cause to leap for joy.

Christiana: I thought one time, as I stood at the gate, because I had knocked and none did answer, that all our labor had been lost, especially when that ugly cur made such a heavy barking against us.

Mercy: But my worst fear was after I saw that you was taken into his favor, and that I was left behind. Now, thought I, it is fulfilled which is written, "Two women shall be grinding at the mill; the one shall be taken, and the other left." (Matt. 24:41). I had much ado to forbear crying out, Undone! And afraid I was to knock anymore; but when I looked up to what was written over the gate, I took courage. I also thought that I must either knock again, or die; so I knocked, but I cannot tell how, for my spirit now struggled between life and death.

Christiana: Can you not tell how you knocked? I am sure your knocks were so earnest that the very sound of them made me start; I thought I never heard such knocking in all my life; I thought you would come in by a violent hand, or take the kingdom by storm. (Matt. 11:12).

Mercy: Alas! to be in my case, who that so was could but have done so? You saw that the door was shut upon me, and there was a most cruel dog thereabout. Who, I say, that was so faint-hearted as I, would not have knocked with all their might? But pray, what said my Lord to my rudeness? Was he not angry with me?

Christiana: When he heard your lumbering noise, he gave a wonderful innocent smile; I believe what you did pleased him well, for he showed no sign to the contrary. But I marvel in my heart why he keeps such a dog: had I known that before, I should not have had heart enough to have ventured myself in this manner. But now we are in, we are in, and I am glad with all my heart.

Mercy: I will ask, if you please, next time he comes down, why he keeps such a filthy cur in his yard; I hope he will not take it amiss.

Do so, said the children, and persuade him to hang him; for we are afraid he will bite us when we go hence.

So at last he came down to them again, and Mercy fell to the ground on her face before him, and worshiped, and said, "Let my Lord accept the sacrifice of praise which I now offer unto him with the calves of my lips."

So he said unto her, Peace be to thee; stand up. But she continued upon her face, and said, "Righteous art thou, O Lord, when I plead with thee; yet let me talk with thee of thy judgments." (Jer. 12:1). Wherefore dost thou keep so cruel a dog in thy yard, at the sight of which such women and children as we are ready to fly from thy gate for fear?

He answered and said, That dog has another owner; he also is kept close in another man's ground, only my pilgrims hear his barking; he belongs to the castle which you see there at a distance, but can come up to the walls of this place. He has frighted many an honest pilgrim from worse to better, by the great voice of his roaring. Indeed, he that owneth him doth not keep him out of any good-will to me or mine, but with intent to keep the pilgrims from coming to me, and that they may be afraid to come and knock at this gate for entrance. Sometimes also he has broken out, and has worried some that I loved; but I take all at present patiently. I also give my pilgrims timely help, so that they are not delivered to his power, to do with them what his doggish nature would prompt him to. But what my purchased one, I trow, hadst thou known never so much beforehand, thou wouldest not have been afraid of a dog. The beggars that go from door to door, will, rather than lose a supposed alms, run the hazard of the bawling, barking, and biting too of a dog; and shall a dog, a dog in another man's yard, a dog whose barking I turn to the profit of pilgrims, keep any from coming to me? I deliver them from the lions, and my darling from the power of the dog. (Psa. 22:21,22).

Mercy: Then said Mercy, I confess my ignorance; I spake what I understood not; I acknowledge that thou doest all things well.

Christiana: Then Christiana began to talk of their journey, and to inquire after the way. So he fed them and washed their feet, and set them in the way of his steps, according as he had dealt with her husband before.

THE SECOND STAGE

So I saw in my dream, that they walked on their way, and had the weather very comfortable to them.

Then Christiana began to sing, saying,

Blessed be the day that I began
A pilgrim for to be;
And blessed also be the man
That thereto moved me.

'Tis true, t was long ere I began
To seek to live forever;
But now I run fast as I can:
'Tis better late than never.

Our tears to joy, our fears to faith,
Are turned, as we see;
Thus our beginning (as one saith)
Shows what our end will be.

Now there was, on the other side of the wall that fenced in the way up which Christiana and her companions were to go, a garden, and that garden belonged to him whose was that barking dog, of whom mention was made before. And some of the fruit-trees that grew in that garden shot their branches over the wall; and being mellow, they that found them did gather them up, and eat of them to their hurt. So Christiana's boys, as boys are apt to do, being pleased with the trees, and with the fruit that hung thereon, did pluck them, and began to eat. Their mother did also chide them for so doing, But still the boys went on.

Well, said she, my sons, you transgress, for that fruit is none of ours; but she did not know that it belonged to the enemy: I'll warrant you, if she had she would have been ready to die for fear. But that passed, and they went on their way. Now, by that they were gone about two bow-shots from the place that led them into the way, they espied two very ill-favored ones coming down apace to meet them. With that, Christiana and Mercy her friend covered themselves with their veils, and so kept on their journey: the children also went on before; so that at last they met together. Then they that came down to meet them, came just up to the women, as if they would embrace them; but Christiana said, stand back, or go peaceably as you should. Yet these two, as men that are deaf, regarded not Christiana's words, but began to lay hands upon them: at that Christiana waxing very wroth, spurned at them with her feet. Mercy also, as well as she could, did what she could to shift them. Christiana again said to them, Stand back, and be gone, for we have no money to lose, being pilgrims, as you see, and such too as live upon the charity of our friends.

Ill-Favored Ones: Then said one of the two men, We make no assault upon you for money, but are come out to tell you, that if you will but grant one small request which we shall ask, we will make women of you forever.

Christiana: Now Christiana, imagining what they should mean, made answer again, We will neither hear, nor regard, nor yield to what you shall ask. We are in haste, and cannot stay; our business is a business of life and death. So again she and her companion made a fresh essay to go past them; but they letted them in their way.

Ill-Favored Ones: And they said, We intend no hurt to your lives; it is another thing we would have.

Christiana: Aye, quoth Christiana, you would have us body and soul, for I know it is for that you are come; but we will die rather upon the spot, than to suffer ourselves to be brought into such snares as shall hazard our well-being hereafter. And with that they both shrieked out, and cried, Murder! Murder! and so put themselves under those laws that are provided for the protection of women. (Deut. 22:25-27). But the men still made their approach upon them, with design to prevail against them. They therefore cried out again.

Now they being, as I said, not far from the gate in at which they came, their voice was heard from whence they were, thither: wherefore some of the house came out, and knowing that it was Christiana's tongue, they made haste to her relief. But by that they were got within sight of them, the women were in a very great scuffle; the children also stood crying by. Then did he that came in for their relief call out to the ruffians, saying, What is that thing you do? Would you make my Lord's people to transgress? He also attempted to take them, but they did make their escape over the wall into the garden of the man to whom the great dog belonged; so the dog became their protector. This Reliever then came up to the women, and asked them how they did. So they answered, We thank thy Prince, pretty well, only we have been somewhat affrighted: we thank thee also for that thou camest in to our help, otherwise we had been overcome.

Reliever: So, after a few more words, this Reliever said as followeth: I marveled much, when you were entertained at the gate above, seeing ye knew that ye were but weak women, that you petitioned not the Lord for a conductor; then might you have avoided these troubles and dangers; for he would have granted you one.

Christiana: Alas! said Christiana, we were so taken with our present blessing, that dangers to come were forgotten by us. Besides, who could have thought, that so near the King's palace there could have lurked such naughty ones? Indeed, it had been well for us had we asked our Lord for one; but since our Lord knew it would be for our profit, I wonder he sent not one along with us.

Reliever: It is not always necessary to grant things not asked for, lest by so doing they become of little esteem; but when they want of a thing is felt, it then comes under, in the eyes of him that feels it, that estimate that properly is its due, and so consequently will be thereafter used. Had my Lord granted you a conductor, you would not either so have bewailed that oversight of yours, in not asking for one, as now you have occasion to do. So all things work for good, and tend to make you more wary.

Christiana: Shall we go back again to my Lord, and confess our folly, and ask one?

Reliever: Your confession of your folly I will present him with. To go back again, you need not, for in all places where you shall come, you will find no want at all; for in every one of my Lord's lodgings, which he has prepared for the reception of his pilgrims, there is sufficient to furnish them against all attempts whatsoever. But, as I said, He will be inquired of by them, to do it for them. (Ezek. 36:37). And 'tis a poor thing that is not worth asking for.

When he had thus said, he went back to his place, and the pilgrims went on their way.

Mercy: Then said Mercy, What a sudden blank is here! I made account that we had been past all danger, and that we should never see sorrow more.

Christiana: Thy innocency, my sister, said Christiana to Mercy, may excuse thee much; but as for me, my fault is so much the greater, for that I saw this danger before I came out of the doors, and yet did not provide for it when provision might have been had. I am much to be blamed.

Mercy: Then said Mercy, How knew you this before you came from home? Pray open to me this riddle.

Christiana: Why, I will tell you. Before I set foot out of doors, one night as I lay in my bed I had a dream about this; for methought I saw two men, as like these as ever any in the world could look, stand at my bed's feet, plotting how they might prevent my salvation. I will tell you their very words. They said, (it was when I was in my troubles,) What shall we do with this woman? for she cries out, waking and sleeping, for forgiveness: if she be sufferet do go on as she begins, we shall lose her as we have lost her husband. This you know might have made me take heed, and have provided when provision might have been had.

Mercy: Well, said Mercy, as by this neglect we have an occasion ministered unto us to behold our own imperfections, so our Lord has taken occasion thereby to make manifest the riches of his grace; for he, as we see, has followed us with unasked kindness, and has delivered us from their hands that were stronger than we, of his mere good pleasure.

Thus now, when they had talked away a little more time, they drew near to a house which stood in the way, which house was built for the relief of pilgrims, as you will find more fully related in the first part of these records of the Pilgrim's Progress. So they drew on towards the house, (the house of the Interpreter;) and when they came to the door, they heard a great talk in the house. Then they gave ear, and heard, as they thought, Christiana mentioned by name; for you must know that there went along, even before her, a talk of her and her children's going on pilgrimage. And this was the most pleasing to them, because they had heard that she was Christian's wife, that woman who was some time ago so unwilling to hear of going on pilgrimage. Thus, therefore, they stood still, and heard the good people within commending her who they little thought stood at the door. At last Christiana knocked, as she had done at the gate before. Now, when she had knocked, there came to the door a young damsel, and opened the door, and looked, and behold, two women were there.

The Damsel: Then said the damsel to them, With whom would you speak in this place?

Christiana: Christiana answered, We understand that this is a privileged place for those that are become pilgrims, and we now at this door are such: wherefore we pray that we may be partakers of that for which we at this time are come; for the day, as thou seest, is very far spent, and we are loth tonight to go any further.

The Damsel: Pray, what may I call your name, that I may tell it to my Lord within.

Christiana: My name is Christiana; I was the wife of that pilgrim that some years ago did travel this way, and these be his four children. This maiden also is my companion, and is going on pilgrimage too.

Innocent: Then Innocent ran in, (for that was her name,) and said to those within, Can you think who is at the door? There is Christiana and her children, and her companion, all waiting for entertainment here. Then they leaped for joy, and went and told their Master. So he came to the door and looking upon her, he said, Art thou that Christiana whom Christian the good man left behind him when he betook himself to a pilgrim's life.

Christiana: I am that woman that was so hard-hearted as to slight my husband's troubles, and that left him to go on in his journey alone, and these are his four children; but now I also am come, for I am convinced that no way is right but this.

Interpreter: Then is fulfilled that which is written of the man that said to his son, "Go work to-day in my vineyard; and he said to his father, I will not: but afterwards repented and went." (Matt. 21:29).

Christiana: Then said Christiana, So be it: Amen. God made it a true saying upon me, and grant that I may be found at the last of him in peace, without spot, and blameless.

Interpreter: But why standest thou thus at the door? Come in, thou daughter of Abraham; we were talking of thee but now, for tidings have come to us before how thou art become a pilgrim. Come, children, come in; come, maiden, come in. So he had them all into the house.

So when they were within, they were bidden to sit down and rest them; the which when they had done, those that attended upon the pilgrims in the house came into the room to see them. And one smiled, and another smiled, and they all smiled for joy that Christiana was become a pilgrim: They also looked upon the boys; they stroked them over their faces with the hand, in token of their kind reception of them: they also carried it lovingly to Mercy, and bid them all welcome into their Master's house.

After a while, because supper was not ready, the Interpreter took them into his Significant Rooms, and showed them what Christian, Christiana's husband, had seen some time before. Here, therefore, they saw the man in the cage, the man and his dream, the man that cut his way through his enemies, and the picture of the biggest of them all, together with the rest of those things that were then so profitable to Christian.

This done, and after those things had been somewhat digested by Christiana and her company, the Interpreter takes them apart again, and has them first into a room where was a man that could look no way but downwards, with a muck-rake in his hand. There stood also one over his head with a celestial crown in his hand, and proffered him that crown for his muck-rake; but the man did neither look up nor regard, but raked to himself the straws, the small sticks, and dust of the floor.

Then said Christiana, I persuade myself that I know somewhat the meaning of this; for this is a figure of a man of this world: is it not, good sir?

Interpreter: Thou hast said right, said he; and his muck-rake doth show his carnal mind. And whereas thou seest him rather give heed to rake up straws and sticks, and the dust of the floor, than to do what He says that calls to him from above with the celestial crown in his hand; it is to show, that heaven is but as a fable to some, and that things here are counted the only things substantial. Now, whereas it was also showed thee that the man could look no way but downwards, it is to let thee know that earthly things, when they are with power upon men's minds, quite carry their hearts away from God.

Christiana: Then said Christiana, O deliver me from this muck-rake. (Prov. 30:8).

Interpreter: That prayer, said the Interpreter, has lain by till it is almost rusty: "Give me not riches," is scarce the prayer of one in ten thousand. Straws, and sticks, and dust, with most, are the great things now looked after.

With that Christiana and Mercy wept, and said, It is, alas! too true.

When the Interpreter had shown them this, he had them into the very best room in the house; a very brave room it was. So he bid them look round about, and see if they could find anything profitable there. Then they looked round and round; for there was nothing to be seen but a very great spider on the wall, and that they overlooked.

Mercy: Then said Mercy, Sir, I see nothing; but Christiana held her peace.

Interpreter: But, said the Interpreter, look again. She therefore looked again, and said, Here is not anything but an ugly spider, who hangs by her hands upon the wall. Then said he, Is there but one spider in all this spacious room? Then the water stood in Christiana's eyes, for she was a woman quick of apprehension; and she said, Yea, Lord, there are more here than one; yea, and spiders whose venom is far more destructive than that which is in her. The Interpreter then looked pleasantly on her, and said, Thou hast said the truth. This made Mercy to blush, and the boys to cover their faces; for they all began now to understand the riddle.

Then said the Interpreter again, "The spider taketh hold with her hands," as you see, "and is in kings' palaces." (Prov. 30:28). And wherefore is this recorded, but to show you, that, how full of the venom of sin soever you be, yet you may, by the hand of Faith, lay hold of and dwell in the best room that belongs to the King's house above?

Christiana: I thought, said Christiana, of something of this; but I could not imagine it at all. I thought that we were like spiders, and that we looked like ugly creatures, in what fine room soever we were: but that by this spider, that venomous and ill-favored creature, we were to learn how to act faith, that came not into my thoughts; and yet she had taken hold with her hands, and, as I see, dwelleth in the best room in the house. God has made nothing in vain.

Then they seemed all to be glad; but the water stood in their eyes; yet they looked one upon another, and also bowed before the Interpreter.

He had them into another room, where were a hen and chickens, and bid them observe a while. So one of the chickens went to the trough to drink, and every time she drank she lifted up her head and her eyes towards heaven. See, said he, what this little chick doth, and learn of her to acknowledge whence your mercies come, by receiving them with looking up. Yet again, said he, observe and look: so they gave heed, and perceived that the hen did walk in a fourfold method towards her chickens:

1. She had a common call, and that she hath all the day long.
2. She had a special call, and that she had but sometimes.
3. She had a brooding note. (Matt. 23:37). And,
4. She had an outcry.

Now, said he, compare this hen to your King and these chickens to his obedient ones; for, answerable to her, he himself hath his methods which he walketh in towards his people. By his common call, he gives nothing; by his special call, he always has something to give; he has also a brooding voice, for them that are under his wing; and he has an outcry, to give the alarm when he seeth the enemy come. I choose, my darlings, to lead you into the room where such things are, because you are women, and they are easy for you.

Christiana: And, sir, said Christiana, pray let us see some more. So he had them into the slaughter-house, where was a butcher killing a sheep; and behold, the sheep was quiet, and took her death patiently. Then said the Interpreter, You must learn of this sheep to suffer and to put up with wrongs without murmurings and complaints. Behold how quietly she takes her death, and, without objecting, she suffereth her skin to be pulled over her ears. Your King doth call you his sheep.

After this he led them into his garden, where was great variety of flowers; and he, said, Do you see all these? So Christiana said, Yes. Then said he again, Behold, the flowers are diverse in stature, in quality, and color, and smell, and virtue; and some are better than others; also, where the gardener has set them, there they stand, and quarrel not one with another.

Again, he had them into his field, which he had sown with wheat and corn: but when they beheld, the tops of all were cut off, and only the straw remained. He said again, This ground was dunged, and ploughed, and sowed, but what shall we do with the crop? Then said Christiana, Burn some, and make muck of the rest. Then said the Interpreter again, Fruit, you see, is that thing you look for;

and for want of that you condemn it to the fire, and to be trodden under foot of men: beware that in this you condemn not yourselves.

Then, as they were coming in from abroad, they espied a little robin with a great spider in his mouth. So the Interpreter said, Look here. So they looked, and Mercy wondered, but Christiana said, What a disparagement is it to such a pretty little bird as the robin-red-breast; he being also a bird above many, that loveth to maintain a kind of sociableness with men! I had thought they had lived upon crumbs of bread, or upon other such harmless matter: I like him worse than I did.

The Interpreter then replied, This robin is an emblem, very apt to set forth some professors by; for to sight they are, as this robin, pretty of note, color, and carriage. They seem also to have a very great love for professors that are sincere; and, above all others, to desire to associate with them, and to be in their company, as if they could live upon the good man's crumbs. They pretend also, that therefore it is that they frequent the house of the godly, and the appointments of the Lord: but when they are by themselves, as the robin, they can catch and gobble up spiders; they can change their diet, drink iniquity, and swallow down sin like water.

So, when they were come again into the house, because supper as yet was not ready, Christiana again desired that the Interpreter would either show or tell some other things that are profitable.

Then the Interpreter began, and said, The fatter the sow is, the more she desires the mire; the fatter the ox is, the more gamesomely he goes to the slaughter; and the more healthy the lustful man is, the more prone he is unto evil. There is a desire in women to go neat and find; and it is a comely thing to be adorned with that which in God's sight is of great price. 'Tis easier watching a night or two, than to sit up a whole year together: so t is easier for one to begin to profess well, than to hold out as he should to the end. Every shipmaster, when in a storm, will willingly cast that overboard which is of the smallest value in the vessel; but who will throw the best out first? None but he that feareth not God. One leak will sink a ship, and one sin will destroy a sinner. He that forgets his friend is ungrateful unto him; but he that forgets his Savior is unmerciful to himself. He that lives in sin, and looks for happiness hereafter, is like him that soweth cockle, and thinks to fill his barn with wheat or barley. If a man would live well, let him fetch his last day to him, and make it always his company-keeper. Whispering, and change of thoughts, prove that sin is in the world. If the world, which God sets light by, is counted a thing of that worth with men, what is heaven, that God commendeth? If the life that is attended with so many troubles, is so loth to be let go by us, what is the life above? Everybody will cry up the goodness of men; but who is there that is, as he should be, affected with the goodness of God? We seldom sit down to meat, but we eat, and leave. So there is in Jesus Christ more merit and righteousness than the whole world has need of.

When the Interpreter had done, he takes them out into his garden again, and had them to a tree whose inside was all rotten and gone, and yet it grew and had leaves. Then said Mercy, What means this? This tree, said he, whose outside is fair, and whose inside is rotten, is that to which many may be compared that are in the garden of God; who with their mouths speak high in behalf of God, but indeed will do nothing for him; whose leaves are fair, but their heart good for nothing but to be tinder for the devil's tinder-box.

Now supper was ready, the table spread, and all things set on the board: so they sat down, and did eat, when one had given thanks. And the Interpreter did usually entertain those that lodged with him with music at meals; so the minstrels played. There was also one that did sing, and a very fine voice he had. His song was this:

"The Lord is only my support,
And he that doth me feed;
How can I then want any thing
Whereof I stand in need?"

When the song and music were ended, the Interpreter asked Christiana what it was that at first did move her thus to betake herself to a pilgrim's life. Christiana answered, First, the loss of my husband came into my mind, at which I was heartily grieved; but all that was but natural affection. Then after that came the troubles and pilgrimage of my husband into my mind, and also how like a churl I had carried it to him as to that. So guilt took hold of my mind, and would have drawn me into the pond, but that opportunely I had a dream of the well-being of my husband, and a letter sent me by the King of that country where my husband dwells, to come to him. The dream and the letter together so wrought upon my mind that they forced me to this way.

Interpreter: But met you with no opposition before you set out of doors?

Christiana: Yes, a neighbor of mine, one Mrs. Timorous: she was akin to him that would have persuaded my husband to go back, for fear of the lions. She also befooled me, for, as she called it, my intended desperate adventure; she also urged what she could to dishearten me from it, the hardships and troubles that my husband met with in the way; but all this I got over pretty well. But a dream that I had of two ill-looking ones, that I thought did plot how to make me miscarry in my journey, that hath troubled me much: yea, it still runs in my mind, and makes me afraid of every one that I meet, lest they should meet me to do me a mischief, and to turn me out of my way. Yea, I may tell my Lord, though I would not have everybody know of it, that between this and the gate by which we got into the way, we were both so sorely assaulted that we were made to cry out murder; and the two that made this assault upon us, were like the two that I saw in my dream.

Then said the Interpreter, Thy beginning is good; thy latter end shall greatly increase. So he addressed himself to Mercy, and said unto her, And what moved thee to come hither, sweet heart?

Mercy: Then Mercy blushed and trembled, and for a while continued silent.

Interpreter: Then said he, Be not afraid; only believe, and speak thy mind.

Mercy: So she began, and said, Truly, sir, my want of experience is that which makes me covet to be in silence, and that also that fills me with fears of coming short at last. I cannot tell of visions and dreams, as my friend Christiana can; nor know I what it is to mourn for my refusing the counsel of those that were good relations.

Interpreter: What was it, then, dear heart, that hath prevailed with thee to do as thou hast done?

Mercy: Why, when our friend here was packing up to be gone from our town, I and another went accidentally to see her. So we knocked at the door and went in. When we were within, and seeing what she was doing, we asked her what was her meaning. She said she was sent for to go to her husband; and then she up and told us how she had seen him in a dream, dwelling in a curious place, among immortals, wearing a crown, playing upon a harp, eating and drinking at his Prince's table, and singing praises to him for bringing him thither, etc. Now, methought, while she was telling these things unto us, my heart burned within me. And I said in my heart, If this be true, I will leave my father and my mother, and the land of my nativity, and will, if I may, go along with Christiana. So I asked her further of the truth of these things, and if she would let me go with her; for I saw now that there was no dwelling, but with the danger of ruin, any longer in our town. But yet I came away with a heavy heart; not for that I was unwilling to come away, but for that so many of my relations were left behind. And I am come with all the desire of my heart, and will go, if I may, with Christiana unto her husband and his King.

Interpreter: Thy setting out is good, for thou hast given credit to the truth; thou art a Ruth, who did, for the love she bare to Naomi and to the Lord her God, leave father and mother, and the land of her nativity, to come out and go with a people she knew not heretofore. "The Lord recompense thy work, and a full reward be given thee of the Lord God of Israel, under whose wings thou art come to trust." (Ruth 2:11,12).

Now supper was ended, and preparation was made for bed; the women were laid singly alone, and the boys by themselves. Now when Mercy was in bed, she could not sleep for joy, for that now her doubts of missing at last were removed further from her than ever they were before. So she lay blessing and praising God, who had such favor for her.

In the morning they arose with the sun, and prepared themselves for their departure; but the Interpreter would have them tarry a while; For, said he, you must orderly go from hence. Then said he to the damsel that first opened unto them, Take them and have them into the garden to the bath, and there wash them and make them clean from the soil which they had gathered by traveling. Then Innocent the damsel took them and led them into the garden, and brought them to the bath; so she told them that there they must wash and be clean, for so her Master would have the women to do that called at his house as they were going on pilgrimage. Then they went in and washed, yea, they and the boys, and all; and they came out of that bath, not only sweet and clean, but also much enlivened and strengthened in their joints. So when they came in, they looked fairer a deal than when they went out to the washing.

When they were returned out of the garden from the bath, the Interpreter took them and looked upon them, and said unto them, "Fair as the moon." Then he called for the seal wherewith they used to be sealed that were washed in his bath. So the seal was brought, and he set his mark upon them, that they might be known in the places whither they were yet to go. Now the seal was the contents and sum of the passover which the children of Israel did eat, (Ex. 13: 8-10), when they came out of the land of Egypt; and the mark was set between their eyes. This seal greatly added to their beauty, for it was an ornament to their faces. It also added to their gravity, and made their countenance more like those of angels.

Then said the Interpreter again to the damsel that waited upon these women, Go into the vestry, and fetch out garments for these people. So she went and fetched out white raiment, and laid it down before him; so he commanded them to put it on: it was fine linen, white and clean. When the women were thus adorned, they seemed to be a terror one to the other; for that they could not see that glory each one had in herself, which they could see in each other. Now therefore they began to esteem each other better than themselves. For, You are fairer than I am, said one; and, You are more comely than I am, said another. The children also stood amazed, to see into what fashion they were brought.

THE THIRD STAGE

The Interpreter then called for a man-servant of his, one Great-heart, and bid him take A sword, and helmet, and shield; and, Take these my daughters, said he, conduct them to the house called Beautiful, at which place they will rest next. So he took his weapons, and went before them; and the Interpreter said, God speed. Those also that belonged to the family, sent them away with many a good wish. So they went on their way, and sang,

This place hath been our second stage:

Here we have heard, and seen
Those good things, that from age to age
To others hid have been.

The dunghill-raker, spider, hen,
The chicken, too, to me
Have taught a lesson: let me then
Conformed to it be.

The butcher, garden, and the field,
The robin and his bait,
Also the rotten tree, doth yield
Me argument of weight,

To move me for to watch and pray,
To strive to be sincere;
To take my cross up day by day,
And serve the Lord with fear.

Now I saw in my dream, that they went on, and Great-Heart before them. So they went, and came to the place where Christian's burden fell off his back and tumbled into a sepulcher. Here then they made a pause; and here also they blessed God. Now, said Christiana, it comes to my mind what was said to us at the gate, to wit, that we should have pardon by word and deed: by word, that is, by the promise; by deed, to wit, in the way it was obtained. What the promise is, of that I know something; but what is it to have pardon by deed, or in the way that it was obtained, Mr. Great-Heart, I suppose you know; wherefore, if you please, let us hear your discourse thereof.

Mr. Great-Heart: Pardon by the deed done, is pardon obtained by someone for another that hath need thereof; not by the person pardoned, but in the way, saith another, in which I have obtained it. So then, to speak to the question more at large, the pardon that you, and Mercy, and these boys have attained, was obtained by another; to wit, by him that let you in at the gate. And he hath obtained it in this double way; he hath performed righteousness to cover you, and spilt his blood to wash you in.

Christiana: But if he parts with his righteousness to us, what will he have for himself?

Mr. Great-Heart: He has more righteousness than you have need of, or than he needeth himself.

Christiana: Pray make that appear.

Mr. Great-Heart: With all my heart: but first I must premise, that he of whom we are now about to speak, is one that has not his fellow: He has two natures in one person, plain to be distinguished, impossible to be divided. Unto each of these natures a righteousness belongeth, and each righteousness is essential to that nature; so that one may as easily cause that nature to be extinct, as to separate its justice or righteousness from it. Of these righteousnesses therefore, we are not made partakers, so as that they, or any of them, should be put upon us, that we might be made just, and live thereby. Besides these, there is a righteousness which this person has, as these two natures are joined in one. And this is not the righteousness of the Godhead, as distinguished from the manhood; nor the righteousness of the manhood, as distinguished from the Godhead; but a righteousness which standeth in the union of both natures, and may properly be called the righteousness that is essential to his being prepared of God to the capacity of the mediatory office, which he was to be entrusted with. If he parts with his first righteousness, he parts with his Godhead; if he parts with his second righteousness, he parts with the purity of his manhood; if he parts with his third, he parts with that perfection that capacitates him to the office of mediation. He has therefore another righteousness, which standeth in performance, or obedience to a revealed will; and that is what he puts upon sinners, and that by which their sins are covered. Wherefore he saith, "As by one man's disobedience many were made sinners, so by the obedience of one shall many be made righteous." (Rom. 5:19).

Christiana: But are the other righteousnesses of no use to us?

Mr. Great-Heart: Yes; for though they are essential to his natures and office, and cannot be communicated unto another, yet it is by virtue of them that the righteousness that justifies is for that purpose efficacious. The righteousness of his Godhead gives virtue to his obedience; the righteousness of his manhood giveth capability to his obedience to justify; and the righteousness that standeth in the union of these two natures to his office, giveth authority to that righteousness to do the work for which it was ordained.

So then here is a righteousness that Christ, as God, has no need of; for he is God without it: Here is a righteousness that Christ, as man, has no need of to make him so; for he is perfect man without it. Again, here is a righteousness that Christ, as God-man, has no need of; for he is perfectly so without it. Here then is a righteousness that Christ, as God, and as God-man, has no need of, with reference to himself, and therefore he can spare it; a justifying righteousness, that he for himself wanteth not, and therefore giveth it away: Hence it is called the gift of righteousness. This righteousness, since Christ Jesus the Lord has made himself under the law, must be given away; for the law doth not only bind him that is under it, to do justly, but to use charity. (Rom. 5:17). Wherefore he must, or ought by the law, if he hath two coats, to give one to him that hath none. Now, our Lord indeed hath two coats, one for himself, and one to spare; wherefore he freely bestows one upon those that have none. And thus, Christiana and Mercy, and the rest of you that are here, doth your pardon come by deed, or by the work of another man. Your Lord Christ is he that worked, and hath given away what he wrought for, to the next poor beggar he meets.

But again, in order to pardon by deed, there must something be paid to God as a price, as well as something prepared to cover us withal. Sin has delivered us up to the just curse of a righteous law: now from this curse we must be justified by way of redemption, a price being paid for the harms we have done; and this is by the blood of your Lord, who came and stood in your place and stead, and died your death for your transgressions: Thus has he ransomed you from your transgressions by blood, and covered your polluted and deformed souls with righteousness, (Rom. 8:34); for the sake of which, God passeth by you and will not hurt you when he comes to judge the world. (Gal. 3:13).

Christiana: This is brave! Now I see that there was something to be learned by our being pardoned by word and deed. Good Mercy, let us labor to keep this in mind: and, my children, do you remember it also. But, sir, was not this it that made my good Christian's burden fall from off his shoulder, and that made him give three leaps for joy?

Mr. Great-Heart: Yes, it was the belief of this that cut those strings that could not be cut by other means; and it was to give him a proof of the virtue of this, that he was suffered to carry his burden to the cross.

Christiana: I thought so; for though my heart was lightsome and joyous before, yet it is ten times more lightsome and joyous now. And I am persuaded by what I have felt, though I have felt but little as yet, that if the most burdened man in the world was here, and did see and believe as I now do, it would make his heart the more merry and blithe.

Mr. Great-Heart: There is not only comfort and the ease of a burden brought to us by the sight and consideration of these, but an endeared affection begot in us by it: for who can, if he doth but once think that pardon comes not only by promise but thus, but be affected with the way and means of his redemption, and so with the man that hath wrought it for him?

Christiana: True; methinks it makes my heart bleed to think that he should bleed for me. Oh, thou loving One: Oh, thou blessed One. Thou deservest to have me; thou hast bought me. Thou deservest to have me all: thou hast paid for me ten thousand times more than I am worth. No marvel that this made the tears stand in my husband's eyes, and that it made him trudge so nimbly on. I am persuaded he wished me with him: but, vile wretch that I was, I let him come all alone. Oh, Mercy, that thy father and mother were here; yea, and Mrs. Timorous also: nay, I wish now with all my heart that here was Madam Wanton too. Surely, surely, their hearts would be affected; nor could the fear of the one, nor the powerful lusts of the other, prevail with them to go home again, and to refuse to become good pilgrims.

Mr. Great-Heart: You speak now in the warmth of your affections; will it, think you, be always thus with you? Besides, this is not communicated to everyone, nor to everyone that did see your Jesus bleed. There were that stood by, and that saw the blood run from the heart to the ground, and yet were so far off this, that instead of lamenting, they laughed at him, and, instead of becoming his disciples, did harden their hearts against him. So that all that you have, my daughters, you have by peculiar impression made by a divine contemplating upon what I have spoken to you. Remember, that 'twas told you, that the hen, by her common call, gives no meat to her chickens. This you have therefore by a special grace.

Now I saw in my dream, that they went on until they were come to the place that Simple, and Sloth, and Presumption, lay and slept in when Christian went by on pilgrimage: and behold, they were hanged up in irons a little way off on the other side.

Mercy: Then said Mercy to him that was their guide and conductor, what are these three men; and for what are they hanged there?

Mr. Great-Heart: These three men were men of very bad qualities; they had no mind to be pilgrims themselves, and whomsoever they could, they hindered. They were sloth and folly themselves, and whomsoever they could persuade they made so too, and withal taught them to presume that they should do well at last. They were asleep when Christian went by; and now you go by, they are hanged.

Mercy: But could they persuade any to be of their opinion?

Mr. Great-Heart: Yes, they turned several out of the way. There was Slow-pace that they persuaded to do as they. They also prevailed with one Short-wind, with one No-heart, with one Linger-after-Lust, and with one Sleepy-head, and with a young woman, her name was Dull, to turn out of the way and become as they. Besides, they brought up an ill report of your Lord, persuading others that he was a hard taskmaster. They also brought up an evil report of the good Land, saying, it was not half so good as some pretended it was. They also began to vilify his servants, and to count the best of them meddlesome, troublesome busybodies. Further, they would call the bread of God husks; the comforts of his children, fancies; the travel and labor of pilgrims, things to no purpose.

Christiana: Nay, said Christiana, if they were such, they shall never be bewailed by me: they have but what they deserve; and I think it is well that they stand so near the highway, that others may see and take warning. But had it not been well if their crimes had been engraved in some plate of iron or brass, and left here where they did their mischiefs, for a caution to other bad men?

Mr. Great-Heart: So it is, as you may well perceive, if you will go a little to the wall.

Mercy: No, no; let them hang, and their names rot, and their crimes live forever against them. I think it a high favor that they were hanged before we came hither: who knows else what they might have done to such poor women as we are? Then she turned it into a song, saying,

"Now then you three hang there, and be a sign
To all that shall against the truth combine.
And let him that comes after, fear this end,
If unto pilgrims he is not a friend.
And thou, my soul, of all such men beware,
That unto holiness opposers are."

Thus they went on till they came to the foot of the hill Difficulty, where again the good Mr. Great-Heart took an occasion to tell them what happened there when Christian himself went by. So he had them first to the spring. Lo, saith he, this is the spring that Christian drank of before he went up this hill: and then it was clear and good; but now it is dirty with the feet of some that are not desirous that pilgrims here should quench their thirst. (Ez. 34:18,19). Thereat Mercy said, And why so envious, trow? But, said their guide, it will do, if taken up and put into a vessel that is sweet and good; for then the dirt will sink to the bottom, and the water come out by itself more clear. Thus therefore Christiana and her companions were compelled to do. They took it up, and put it into an earthen pot, and so let it stand till the dirt was gone to the bottom, and then they drank thereof.

Next he showed them the two by-ways that were at the foot of the hill, where Formality and Hypocrisy lost themselves. And, said he, these are dangerous paths. Two were here cast away when Christian came by; and although, as you see these ways are since stopped up with chains, posts, and a ditch, yet there are those that will choose to adventure here rather than take the pains to go up this hill.

Christiana: "The way of transgressors is hard." (Prov. 13:15). It is a wonder that they can get into these ways without danger of breaking their necks.

Mr. Great-Heart: They will venture: yea, if at any time any of the King's servants do happen to see them, and do call upon them, and tell them that they are in the wrong way, and do bid them beware of the danger, then they railingly return them answer, and say, "As for the word that thou hast spoken unto us in the name of the King, we will not hearken unto thee; but we will certainly do whatsoever thing goeth out of our own mouths." (Jer. 44:16,17). Nay, if you look a little further, you shall see that these ways are made cautionary enough, not only by these posts, and ditch, and chain, but also by being hedged up: yet they will choose to go there.

Christiana: They are idle; they love not to take pains; up-hill way is unpleasant to them. So it is fulfilled unto them as it is written, "The way of the slothful man is full of thorns." (Prov. 15:19). Yea, they will rather choose to walk upon a snare than to go up this hill, and the rest of this way to the city.

Then they set forward, and began to go up the hill, and up the hill they went. But before they got to the top, Christiana began to pant, and said, I dare say this is a breathing hill; no marvel if they that love their ease more than their souls choose to themselves a smoother way.

Then said Mercy, I must sit down: also the least of the children began to cry. Come, come, said Great-Heart, sit not down here; for a little above is the Prince's arbor. Then he took the little boy by the hand, and led him up thereto.

When they were come to the arbor, they were very willing to sit down, for they were all in a pelting heat. Then said Mercy, "How sweet is rest to them that labor." (Matt. 11:28); and how good is the Prince of pilgrims to provide such resting-places for them! Of this arbor I have heard much; but I never saw it before. But here let us beware of sleeping; for, as I have heard, it cost poor Christian dear.

Then said Mr. Great-Heart to the little ones, Come, my pretty boys, how do you do? What think you now of going on pilgrimage? Sir, said the least, I was almost beat out of heart; but I thank you for lending me a hand at my need. And I remember now what my mother hath told me, namely, that the way to heaven is as a ladder, and the way to hell is as down a hill. But I had rather go up the ladder to life, than down the hill to death.

Then said Mercy, But the proverb is, "To go down the hill is easy." But James said, (for that was his name,) The day is coming when, in my opinion, when going down the hill will be the hardest of all. 'Tis a good boy, said his master; thou hast given her a right answer. Then Mercy smiled, but the little boy did blush.

Christiana: Come, said Christiana, will you eat a bit to sweeten your mouths, while you sit here to rest your legs? for I have here a piece of pomegranate which Mr. Interpreter put into my hand just when I came out of his door; he gave me also a piece of an honeycomb, and a little bottle of spirits. I thought he gave you something, said Mercy, because he called you aside. Yes, so he did, said the other; but, said Christiana, it shall be still as I said it should, when at first we came from home; thou shalt be a sharer in all the good that I have, because thou so willingly didst become my companion. Then she gave to them, and they did eat, both Mercy and the boys. And said Christiana to Mr. Great-Heart, Sir, will you do as we? But he answered, You are going on pilgrimage, and presently I shall return; much good may what you have do you: at home I eat the same every day.

THE FOURTH STAGE

Now when they had eaten and drank, and had chatted a little longer, their guide said to them, The day wears away; if you think good, let us prepare to be going. So they got up to go, and the little boys went before; But Christiana forgot to take her bottle of spirits with her, so she sent her little boy back to fetch it. Then said Mercy, I think this is a losing place: here Christian lost his roll, and here Christiana left her bottle behind her. Sir, what is the cause of this? So their guide made answer, and said, The cause is sleep, or forgetfulness: some sleep when they should keep awake, and some forget when they should remember; and this is the very cause why often, at the resting-places, some pilgrims in some things come off losers. Pilgrims should watch, and remember what they have already received, under their greatest enjoyments; but for want of doing so, oftentimes their rejoicing ends in tears, and their sunshine in a cloud: witness the story of Christian at this place.

When they were come to the place where Mistrust and Timorous met Christian, to persuade him to go back for fear of the lions, they perceived as it were a stage, and before it, towards the road, a broad plate with a copy of verses written thereon, and underneath the reason of raising up that stage in that place rendered. The verses were,

"Let him that sees this stage, take heed
Unto his heart and tongue;
Lest, if he do not, here he speed
As some have long agone."

The words underneath the verses were, "This stage was built to punish those upon, who, through timorousness or mistrust, shall be afraid to go further on pilgrimage. Also, on this stage both Mistrust and Timorous were burned through the tongue with a hot iron, for endeavoring to hinder Christian on his journey."

Then said Mercy, This is much like to the saying of the Beloved: "What shall be given unto thee, or what shall be done unto thee, thou false tongue? Sharp arrows of the mighty, with coals of juniper. (Ps. 120:3,4).

So they went on till they came within sight of the lions. Now Mr. Great-Heart was a strong man, so he was not afraid of a lion: But yet when they were come up to the place where the lions were, the boys, that went before, were now glad to cringe behind, for they were afraid of the lions; so they stepped back, and went behind. At this their guide smiled, and said, How now, my boys; do you love to go before when no danger doth approach, and love to come behind so soon as the lions appear?

Now, as they went on, Mr. Great-heart drew his sword, with intent to make a way for the pilgrims in spite of the lions. Then there appeared one that, it seems, had taken upon him to back the lions; and he said to the pilgrims' guide, What is the cause of your coming hither? Now the name of that man was Grim, or Bloody-man because of his slaying of pilgrims; and he was of the race of the giants.

Mr. Great-Heart: Then said the pilgrims' guide, These women and children are going on pilgrimage, and this is the way they must go; and go it they shall, in spite of thee and the lions.

Grim: This is not their way, neither shall they go therein. I am come forth to withstand them, and to that end will back the lions.

Now, to say the truth, by reason of the fierceness of the lions, and of the grim carriage of him that did back them, this way had of late lain much unoccupied, and was almost grown over with grass.

Christiana: Then said Christiana, Though the highways have been unoccupied heretofore, and though the travelers have been made in times past to walk through by-paths, it must not be so now I am risen, now I am risen a mother in Israel. (Judges 5:6,7).

Grim: Then he swore by the lions that it should; and therefore bid them turn aside, for they should not have passage there.

But Great-Heart their guide made first his approach unto Grim, and laid so heavily on him with his sword that he forced him to retreat.

Grim: Then said he that attempted to back the lions, Will you slay me upon mine own ground?

Mr. Great-Heart: It is the King's highway that we are in, and in this way it is that thou hast placed the lions; but these women, and these children, though weak, shall hold on their way in spite of thy lions. And with that he gave him again a downright blow, and brought him upon his knees. With this blow also he broke his helmet, and with the next he cut off an arm. Then did the giant roar so hideously that his voice frightened the women, and yet they were glad to see him lie sprawling upon the ground. Now the lions were chained, and so of themselves could do nothing. Wherefore, when old Grim, that intended to back them, was dead, Mr. Great-Heart said to the pilgrims, Come now, and follow me, and no hurt shall happen to you from the lions. They therefore went on, but the women trembled as they passed by them; the boys also looked as if they would die; but they all got by without further hurt.

Now, when they were within sight of the Porter's lodge, they soon came up unto it; but they made the more haste after this to go thither, because it is dangerous traveling there in the night. So when they were come to the gate, the guide knocked, and the Porter cried, Who is there? But as soon as the guide had said, It is I, he knew his voice, and came down, for the guide had oft before that come thither as a conductor of pilgrims. When he was come down, he opened the gate; and seeing the guide standing just before it, (for he saw not the women, for they were behind him,) he said unto him, How now, Mr. Great-Heart, what is your business here so late at night? I have brought, said he, some pilgrims hither, where, by my Lord's commandment, they must lodge: I had been here some time ago, had I not been opposed by the giant that did use to back the lions. But I, after a long and tedious combat with him, have cut him off, and have brought the pilgrims hither in safety.

The Porter: Will you not go in, and stay till morning?

Mr. Great-Heart: No, I will return to my Lord tonight.

Christiana: O, sir, I know not how to be willing you should leave us in our pilgrimage: you have been so faithful and loving to us, you have fought so stoutly for us, you have been so hearty in counseling of us, that I shall never forget your favor towards us.

Mercy: Then said Mercy, O that we might have thy company to our journey's end! How can such poor women as we hold out in a way so full of troubles as this way is, without a friend and defender?

James: Then said James, the youngest of the boys, Pray, sir, be persuaded to go with us, and help us, because we are so weak, and the way so dangerous as it is.

Mr. Great-Heart: I am at my Lord's commandment; if he shall allot me to be your guide quite through, I will willingly wait upon you. But here you failed at first; for when he bid me come thus far with you, then you should have begged me of him to have gone quite through with you, and he would have granted your request. However, at present I must withdraw; and so, good Christiana, Mercy, and my brave children, adieu.

Then the Porter, Mr. Watchful, asked Christiana of her country, and of her kindred. And she said, I came from the city of Destruction. I am a widow woman, and my husband is dead, his name was Christian, the pilgrim. How! said the Porter, was he your husband? Yes, said she, and these are his children and this, pointing to Mercy, is one of my town's-women. Then the Porter rang his bell, as at such times he is wont, and there come to the door one of the damsels, whose name was Humble-Mind; and to her the Porter said, Go tell it within, that Christiana, the wife of Christian, and her children, are come hither on pilgrimage. She went in, therefore, and told it. But oh, what noise for gladness was there within when the damsel did but drop that out of her mouth!

So they came with haste to the Porter, for Christiana stood still at the door. Then some of the most grave said unto her, Come in, Christiana, come in, thou wife of that good man; come in, thou blessed woman, come in, with all that are with thee. So she went in, and they followed her that were her children and companions. Now when they were gone in, they were had into a large room, where they were bidden to sit down: so they sat down, and the chief of the house were called to see and welcome the guests. Then they came in, and understanding who they were, did salute each other with a kiss, and said, Welcome, ye vessels of the grace of God; welcome to us, your friends.

Now, because it was somewhat late, and because the pilgrims were weary with their journey, and also made faint with the sight of the fight, and of the terrible lions, they desired, as soon as might be, to prepare to go to rest. Nay, said those of the family, refresh yourselves first with a morsel of meat; for they had prepared for them a lamb, with the accustomed sauce belonging thereto, (Ex. 12:21; John 1:29); for the Porter had heard before of their coming, and had told it to them within. So when they had supped, and ended their prayer with a psalm, they desired they might go to rest.

But let us, said Christiana, if we may be so bold as to choose, be in that chamber that was my husband's when he was here; so they had them up thither, and they all lay in a room. When they were at rest, Christiana and Mercy entered into discourse about things that were convenient.

Christiana: Little did I think once, when my husband went on pilgrimage, that I should ever have followed him.

Mercy: And you as little thought of lying in his bed, and in his chamber to rest, as you do now.

Christiana: And much less did I ever think of seeing his face with comfort, and of worshiping the Lord the King with him; and yet now I believe I shall.

Mercy: Hark, don't you hear a noise?

Christiana: Yes, it is, as I believe, a noise of music, for joy that we are here.

Mercy: Wonderful! Music in the house, music in the heart, and music also in heaven, for joy that we are here! Thus they talked a while, and then betook themselves to sleep.

So in the morning when they were awake, Christiana said to Mercy, What was the matter that you did laugh in your sleep to-night? I suppose you were in a dream.

Mercy: So I was, and a sweet dream it was; but are you sure I laughed?

Christiana: Yes, you laughed heartily; but prithee, Mercy, tell me thy dream.

Mercy: I was a dreaming that I sat all alone in a solitary place, and was bemoaning of the hardness of my heart. Now I had not sat there long but methought many were gathered about me to see me, and to hear what it was that I said. So they hearkened, and I went on bemoaning the hardness of my heart. At this, some of them laughed at me, some called me fool, and some began to thrust me about. With that, methought I looked up and saw one coming with wings towards me. So he came directly to me, and said, Mercy, what aileth thee? Now when he had heard me make my complaint, he said, Peace be to thee; he also wiped my eyes with his handkerchief, and clad me in silver and gold. (Ez. 16:8-11). He put a chain about my neck, and ear-rings in mine ears, and a beautiful crown upon my head. Then he took me by the hand, and said, Mercy, come after me. So he went up, and I followed till we came at a golden gate. Then he knocked; and when they within had opened, the man went in, and I followed him up to a throne, upon which one sat; and he said to me, Welcome, daughter. The place looked bright and twinkling, like the stars, or rather like the sun, and I thought that I saw your husband there; so I awoke from my dream. But did I laugh?

Christiana: Laugh! aye, and well you might to see yourself so well. For you must give me leave to tell you that it was a good dream; and that, as you have begun to find the first part true, so you shall find the second at last. "God speaks once, yea, twice, yet man perceiveth it not; in a dream, in a vision of the night, when deep sleep falleth upon men, in slumberings upon the bed." (Job 33:14,15). We need not, when abed, to lie awake to talk with God; he can visit us while we sleep, and cause us then to hear his voice. Our heart oftentimes wakes when we sleep, and God can speak to that, either by words, by proverbs, by signs and similitudes, as well as if one was awake.

Mercy: Well, I am glad of my dream; for I hope ere long to see it fulfilled, to the making me laugh again.

Christiana: I think it is now high time to rise, and to know what we must do.

Mercy: Pray, if they invite us to stay a while, let us willingly accept of the proffer. I am the more willing to stay a while here, to grow better acquainted with these maids: methinks Prudence, Piety, and Charity, have very comely and sober countenances.

Christiana: We shall see what they will do.

So when they were up and ready, they came down, and they asked one another of their rest, and if it was comfortable or not.

Mercy: Very good, said Mercy: it was one of the best night's lodgings that ever I had in my life.

Then said Prudence and Piety, If you will be persuaded to stay here a while, you shall have what the house will afford.

Charity: Aye, and that with a very good will, said Charity. So they consented, and stayed there about a month or above, and became very profitable one to another. And because Prudence would see how Christiana had brought up her children, she asked leave of her to catechize them. So she gave her free consent. Then she began with her youngest, whose name was James.

Prudence: And she said, Come, James, canst thou tell me who made thee?

James: God the Father, God the Son, and God the Holy Ghost.

Prudence: Good boy. And canst thou tell who saved thee?

James: God the Father, God the Son, and God the Holy Ghost.

Prudence: Good boy still. But how doth God the Father save thee?

James: By his grace.

Prudence: How doth God the Son save thee?

James: By his righteousness, death and blood, and life.

Prudence: And how doth God the Holy Ghost save thee?

James: By his illumination, by his renovation, and by his preservation.

Then said Prudence to Christiana, You are to be commended for thus bringing up your children. I suppose I need not ask the rest these questions, since the youngest of them can answer them so well. I will therefore now apply myself to the next youngest.

Prudence: Then she said, Come, Joseph, (for his name was Joseph,) will you let me catechize you?

Joseph: With all my heart.

Prudence: What is man? Joseph: A reasonable creature, so made by God, as my brother said.

Prudence: What is supposed by this word, saved?

Joseph: That man, by sin, has brought himself into a state of captivity and misery.

Prudence: What is supposed by his being saved by the Trinity?

Joseph: That sin is so great and mighty a tyrant that none can pull us out of its clutches but God; and that God is so good and loving to man, as to pull him indeed out of this miserable state.

Prudence: What is God's design in saving poor men?

Joseph: The glorifying of his name, of his grace, and justice, etc., and the everlasting happiness of his creature.

Prudence: Who are they that will be saved?

Joseph: They that accept of his salvation.

Prudence: Good boy, Joseph; thy mother hath taught thee well, and thou hast hearkened unto what she has said unto thee.

Then said Prudence to Samuel, who was the eldest but one, Prudence: Come, Samuel, are you willing that I should catechize you?

Samuel: Yes, forsooth, if you please.

Prudence: What is heaven?

Samuel: A place and state most blessed, because God dwelleth there.

Prudence: What is hell?

Samuel: A place and state most woeful, because it is the dwelling-place of sin, the devil, and death.

Prudence: Why wouldst thou go to heaven?

Samuel: That I may see God, and serve him without weariness; that I may see Christ, and love him everlastingly; that I may have that fullness of the Holy Spirit in me which I can by no means here enjoy.

Prudence: A very good boy, and one that has learned well.

Then she addressed herself to the eldest, whose name was Matthew; and she said to him, Come, Matthew, shall I also catechize you?

Matthew: With a very good will.

Prudence: I ask then, if there was ever anything that had a being antecedent to or before God?

Matthew: No, for God is eternal; nor is there anything, excepting himself, that had a being until the beginning of the first day. For in six days the Lord made heaven and earth, the sea, and all that in them is.

Prudence: What do you think of the Bible?

Matthew: It is the holy word of God.

Prudence: Is there nothing written therein but what you understand?

Matthew: Yes, a great deal. Prudence: What do you do when you meet with places therein that you do not understand?

Matthew: I think God is wiser than I. I pray also that he will please to let me know all therein that he knows will be for my good.

Prudence: How believe you as touching the resurrection of the dead?

Matthew: I believe they shall rise the same that was buried; the same in nature, though not in corruption. And I believe this upon a double account: first, because God has promised it; secondly, because he is able to perform it.

Then said Prudence to the boys, You must still hearken to your mother; for she can teach you more. You must also diligently give ear to what good talk you shall hear from others: for your sakes do they speak good things. Observe also, and that with carefulness, what the heavens and the earth do teach you; but especially be much in the meditation of that book which was the cause of your father's becoming a pilgrim. I, for my part, my children, will teach you what I can while you are here, and shall be glad if you will ask me questions that tend to godly edifying.

Now by that these pilgrim's had been at this place a week, Mercy had a visitor that pretended some good-will unto her, and his name was Mr. Brisk; a man of some breeding, and that pretended to religion, but a man that stuck very close to the world. So he came once or twice, or more, to Mercy, and offered love unto her. Now Mercy was of a fair countenance, and therefore the more alluring.

Her mind also was to be always busying of herself in doing; for when she had nothing to do for herself, she would be making hose and garments for others, and would bestow them upon those that had need. And Mr. Brisk not knowing where or how she disposed of what she made, seemed to be greatly taken, for that he found her never idle. I will warrant her a good housewife, quoth he to himself.

Mercy then revealed the business to the maidens that were of the house, and inquired of them concerning him, for they did know him better than she. So they told her that he was a very busy young man, and one who pretended to religion, but was, as they feared, a stranger to the power of that which is good.

Nay then, said Mercy, I will look no more on him; for I purpose never to have a clog to my soul.

Prudence then replied, that there needed no matter of great discouragement to be given to him; her continuing so as she had begun to do for the poor, would quickly cool his courage.

So the next time he comes he finds her at her old work, making things for the poor. Then said he, What, always at it? Yes, said she, either for myself or for others. And what canst thou earn a day? said he. I do these things, said she, that I may be rich in good works, laying up in store for myself a good foundation against the time to come, that I may lay hold on eternal life. (1 Tim. 6:17-19). Why, prithee, what doest thou with them? said he. Clothe the naked, said she. With that his countenance fell. So he forbore to come at her again. And when he was asked the reason why, he said, that Mercy was a pretty lass, but troubled with ill conditions.

When he had left her, Prudence said, Did I not tell thee that Mr. Brisk would soon forsake thee? yea, he will rise up an ill report of thee; for, notwithstanding his pretence to religion, and his seeming love to Mercy, yet Mercy and he are of tempers so different that I believe they will never come together.

Mercy: I might have had husbands before now, though I spoke not of it to any; but they were such as did not like my conditions, though never did any of them find fault with my person. So they and I could not agree.

Prudence: Mercy in our days is but little set by any further than as to its name: the practice which is set forth by thy conditions, there are but few that can abide.

Mercy: Well, said Mercy, if nobody will have me, I will die unmarried, or my conditions shall be to me as a husband: for I cannot change my nature; and to have one who lies cross to me in this, that I purpose never to admit of as long as I live. I had a sister named Bountiful, that was married to one of these churls, but he and she could never agree; but because my sister was resolved to do as she had begun, that is, to show kindness to the poor, therefore her husband first cried her down at the cross, and then turned her out of his doors.

Prudence: And yet he was a professor, I warrant you?

Mercy: Yes, such a one as he was, and of such as he the world is now full: but I am for none of them all.

Now Matthew, the eldest son of Christiana, fell sick, and his sickness was sore upon him, for he was much pained in his bowels, so that he was with it at times pulled, as it were, both ends together. There dwelt also not far from thence one Mr. Skill, an ancient and well-approved physician. So Christiana desired it, and entered the room, and had a little observed the boy, he concluded that he was sick of the gripes. Then he said to his mother, What diet has Matthew of late fed upon? Diet! said Christiana, nothing but what is wholesome. The physician answered, This boy has been tampering with something that lies in his stomach undigested, and that will not away without means. And I tell you he must be purged, or else he will die.

Samuel: Then said Samuel, Mother, what was that which my brother did gather up and eat as soon as we were come from the gate that is at the head of this way? You know that there was an orchard on the left hand, on the other side of the wall, and some of the trees hung over the wall, and my brother did pluck and eat.

Christiana: True, my child, said Christiana, he did take thereof, and did eat: naughty boy as he was, I chid him, and yet he would eat thereof.

Mr. Skill: I knew he had eaten something that was not wholesome food; and that food, to wit, that fruit, is even the most hurtful of all. It is the fruit of Beelzebub's orchard. I do marvel that none did warn you of it; many have died thereof.

Christiana: Then Christiana began to cry; and she said, Oh, naughty boy! and Oh, careless mother! what shall I do for my son?

Mr. Skill: Come, do not be too much dejected; the boy may do well again, but he must purge and vomit.

Christiana: Pray, sir, try the utmost of your skill with him, whatever it costs.

Mr. Skill: Nay, I hope I shall be reasonable. So he made him a purge, but it was too weak; it was said it was made of the blood of a goat, the ashes of a heifer, and some of the juice of hyssop. (Heb. 9:13, 19; 10: 1-4). When Mr. Skill had seen that that purge was too weak, he made one to the purpose. It was made ex *carne et sanguine Christi*,[1] (John 6:54-57; Heb. 9:14); (you know physicians give strange medicines to their patients:) and it was made into pills, with a promise or two, and a proportional quantity of salt. (Mark 9:49). Now, he was to take them three at a time, fasting, in half a quarter of a pint of the tears of repentance. (Zech. 12:10).

When this potion was prepared, and brought to the boy, he was loth to take it, though torn with the gripes as if he should be pulled in pieces. Come, come, said the physician, you must take it. It goes against my stomach, said the boy. I must have you take it, said his mother. I shall vomit it up again, said the boy. Pray, sir, said Christiana to Mr. Skill, how does it taste? It has no ill taste, said the doctor; and with that she touched one of the pills with the tip of her tongue. Oh, Matthew, said she, this potion is sweeter than honey. If thou lovest thy mother, if thou lovest thy brothers, if thou lovest Mercy, if thou lovest thy life, take it. So, with much ado, after a short prayer for the blessing of God upon it, he took it, and it wrought kindly with him. It caused him to purge; it caused him to sleep, and to rest quietly; it put him into a fine heat and breathing sweat, and did quite rid him of his gripes. So in a little time he got up, and walked about with a staff, and would go from room to room, and talk with Prudence, Piety, and Charity, of his distemper, and how he was healed.

[1] Of the flesh and blood of Christ.

So when the boy was healed, Christiana asked Mr. Skill, saying, Sir, what will content you for your pains and care to and of my child? And he said, You must pay the master of the College of Physicians, (Heb. 13:11-15), according to rules made in that case and provided.

Christiana: But, sir, said she, what is this pill good for else?

Mr. Skill: It is a universal pill; it is good against all the diseases that pilgrims are incident to; and when it is well prepared, it will keep good, time out of mind.

Christiana: Pray, sir, make me up twelve boxes of them; for if I can get these, I will never take other physic.

Mr. Skill: These pills are good to prevent diseases, as well as to cure when one is sick. Yea, I dare say it, and stand to it, that if a man will but use this physic as he should, it will make him live forever. (John 6:51). But, good Christiana, thou must give these pills no other way but as I have prescribed; for if you do, they will do no good. So he gave unto Christiana physic for herself, and her boys, and for Mercy; and bid Matthew take heed how he ate any more green plums; and kissed them, and went his way.

It was told you before, that Prudence bid the boys, that if at any time they would, they should ask her some questions that might be profitable and she would say something to them.

Matthew: Then Matthew, who had been sick, asked her, why for the most part physic should be bitter to our palates.

Prudence: To show how unwelcome the word of God and the effects thereof are to a carnal heart.

Matthew: Why does physic, if it does good, purge, and cause to vomit?

Prudence: To show that the word, when it works effectually, cleanseth the heart and mind. For look, what the one doth to the body, the other doth to the soul.

Matthew: What should we learn by seeing the flame of our fire go upwards, and by seeing the beams and sweet influences of the sun strike downwards?

Prudence: By the going up of the fire, we are taught to ascend to heaven by fervent and hot desires. And by the sun sending his heat, beams, and sweet influences downwards, we are taught the Savior of the world, though high, reaches down with his grace and love to us below.

Matthew: Whence have the clouds their water?

Prudence: Out of the sea.

Matthew: What may we learn from that?

Prudence: That ministers should fetch their doctrine from God.

Matthew: Why do they empty themselves upon the earth?

Prudence: To show that ministers should give out what they know of God to the world.

Matthew: Why is the rainbow caused by the sun?

Prudence: To show that the covenant of God's grace is confirmed to us in Christ.

Matthew: Why do the springs come from the sea to us through the earth?

Prudence: To show that the grace of God comes to us through the body of Christ.

Matthew: Why do some of the springs rise out of the tops of high hills?

Prudence: To show that the Spirit of grace shall spring up in some that are great and mighty, as well as in many that are poor and low.

Matthew: Why doth the fire fasten upon the candle-wick?

Prudence: To show that unless grace doth kindle upon the heart, there will be no true light of life in us.

Matthew: Why are the wick, and tallow and all, spent to maintain the light of the candle?

Prudence: To show that body and soul, and all, should be at the service of, and spend themselves to maintain in good condition that grace of God that is in us.

Matthew: Why doth the pelican pierce her own breast with her bill?

Prudence: To nourish her young ones with her blood, and thereby to show that Christ the blessed so loved his young, (his people,) as to save them from death by his blood.

Matthew: What may one learn by hearing the cock to crow?

Prudence: Learn to remember Peter's sin, and Peter's repentance. The cock's crowing shows also, that day is coming on: let, then, the crowing of the cock put thee in mind of that last and terrible day of judgment.

Now about this time their month was out; wherefore they signified to those of the house, that it was convenient for them to up and be going. Then said Joseph to his mother, It is proper that you forget not to send to the house of Mr. Interpreter, to pray him to grant that Mr. Great-Heart should be sent unto us, that he may be our conductor for the rest of the way. Good boy, said she, I had almost forgot. So she drew up a petition, and prayed Mr. Watchful the porter to send it by some fit man to her good friend Mr. Interpreter; who, when it was come, and he had seen the contents of the petition, said to the messenger, Go, tell them that I will send him.

When the family where Christiana was, saw that they had a purpose to go forward, they called the whole house together, to give thanks to their King for sending of them such profitable guests as these. Which done, they said unto Christiana, And shall we not show thee something, as our custom is to do to pilgrims, on which thou mayest meditate when thou art upon the way? So they took Christiana, her children, and Mercy, into the closet, and showed them one of the apples that Eve ate of, and that she also did give to her husband, and that for the eating of which they were both turned out of paradise, and asked her what she thought that was. Then Christiana said, It is food or poison, I know not which. So they opened the matter to her, and she held up her hands and wondered. (Gen. 3:6; Rom. 7:24).

Then they had her to a place, and showed her Jacob's ladder. (Gen. 28:12). Now at that time there were some angels ascending upon it. So Christiana looked and looked to see the angels go up: so did the rest of the company. Then they were going into another place, to show them something else; but James said to his mother, Pray, bid them stay here a little longer, for this is a curious sight. So they turned again, and stood feeding their eyes with this so pleasant a prospect.

After this, they had them into a place where did hang up a golden anchor. So they bid Christiana take it down; for said they, You shall have it with you, for it is of absolute necessity that you should, that you may lay hold of that within the veil, (Heb. 6:19), and stand steadfast in case you should meet with turbulent weather, (Joel 3:16): so they were glad thereof.

Then they took them, and had them to the mount upon which Abraham our father offered up Isaac his son, and showed them the altar, the wood, the fire, and the knife, for they remain to be seen to this very day. (Gen. 22:9). When they had seen it, they held up their hands, and blessed themselves, and said, Oh, what a man for love to his Master, and for denial to himself, was Abraham!

After they had showed them all these things, Prudence took them into a dining room, where stood a pair of excellent virginals;[2] so she played upon them, and turned what she had showed them into this excellent song, saying,

"Eve's apple we have showed you;
Of that be you aware:
You have seen Jacob's ladder too,
Upon which angels are.
An anchor you received have;
But let not these suffice,
Until with Abram you have gave
Your best, a sacrifice."

[2] A musical instrument.

Now, about this time, one knocked at the door; so the Porter opened, and behold, Mr. Great-Heart was there. But when he was come in, what joy was there! for it came now afresh again into their minds, how but a while ago he had slain old Grim Bloody-man the giant, and had delivered them from the lions.

Then said Mr. Great-Heart to Christiana and to Mercy, My Lord has sent each of you a bottle of wine, and also some parched corn, together with a couple of pomegranates; he has also sent the boys some figs and raisins; to refresh you in your way.

Then they addressed themselves to their journey, and Prudence and Piety went along with them. When they came to the gate, Christiana asked the Porter if any of late went by. He said, No; only one, some time since, who also told me, that of late there had been a great robbery committed on the King's highway as you go. But, said he, the thieves are taken, and will shortly be tried for their lives. Then Christiana and Mercy were afraid; but Matthew said, Mother, fear nothing, as long as Mr. Great-Heart is to go with us, and to be our conductor.

Then said Christiana to the Porter, Sir, I am much obliged to you for all the kindnesses that you have showed to me since I came hither; and also for that you have been so loving and kind to my children. I know not how to gratify your kindness; wherefore, pray, as a token of my respect to you, accept of this small mite. So she put a gold angel[3] in his hand; and he made her a low obeisance, and said, "Let thy garments be always white; and let thy head want no ointment." (Eccles. 9:8). Let Mercy live and not die, and let not

[3] A gold angel was a coin of the value of ten shillings sterling and according to the comparative value of money in Bunyan's time, equal at least to a guinea at the present time.

her works be few. (Deut. 33:6). And to the boys he said, Do you fly youthful lusts, and follow after godliness with them that are grave and wise, (2 Tim. 2:22): so shall you put gladness into your mother's heart, and obtain praise of all that are sober-minded. So they thanked the Porter, and departed.

THE FIFTH STAGE

Now I saw in my dream, that they went forward until they were come to the brow of the Hill; where Piety, bethinking herself, cried out, Alas, I have forgot what I intended to bestow upon Christiana and her companions: I will go back and fetch it. So she ran and fetched it. While she was gone, Christiana thought she heard, in a grove a little way off on the right hand, a most curious melodious note, with words much like these:

"Through all my life thy favor is
So frankly showed to me,
That in thy House for evermorez
My dwelling-place shall be."

And listening still, she thought she heard another answer it, saying,

"For why? The Lord our God is good;
His mercy is forever sure;
His truth at all times firmly stood,
And shall from age to age endure."

So Christiana asked Prudence who it was that made those curious notes. (Song 2:11,12). They are, answered she, our country birds: they sing these notes but seldom, except it be at the spring, when the flowers appear, and the sun shines warm, and then you may hear them all day long. I often, said she, go out to hear them; we also oft-times keep them tame in our house. They are very fine company for us when we are melancholy: also they make the woods, and groves, and solitary places, places desirable to be in.

By this time Piety was come again. So she said to Christiana, Look here, I have brought thee a scheme of all those things that thou hast seen at our house, upon which thou mayest look when thou findest thyself forgetful, and call those things again to remembrance for thy edification and comfort.

Now they began to go down the hill into the Valley of Humiliation. It was a steep hill, and the way was slippery; but they were very careful; so they got down pretty well. When they were down in the valley, Piety said to Christiana, This is the place where Christian your husband met with the foul fiend Apollyon, and where they had that dreadful fight that they had: I know you cannot but have heard thereof. But be of good courage; as long as you have here Mr. Great-Heart to be your guide and conductor, we hope you will fare the better. So when these two had committed the pilgrims unto the conduct of their guide, he went forward, and they went after.

Mr. Great-Heart: Then said Mr. Great-Heart, We need not be so afraid of this valley, for here is nothing to hurt us, unless we procure it to ourselves. It is true, Christian did here meet with Apollyon, with whom he had also a sore combat: but that fray was the fruit of those slips that he got in his going down the hill: for they that get slips there, must look for combats here. And hence it is, that this valley has got so hard a name. For the common people, when they hear that some frightful thing has befallen such an one in such a place, are of opinion that that place is haunted with some foul fiend, or evil spirit; when, alas! it is for the fruit of their doing, that such things do befall them there. This Valley of Humiliation is of itself as fruitful a place as any the crow flies over; and I am persuaded, if we could hit upon it, we might find somewhere hereabouts something that might give us an account why Christian was so hardly beset in this place.

Then said James to his mother, Lo, yonder stands a pillar, and it looks as if something was written thereon; let us go and see what it is. So they went and found there written, "Let Christian's slips, before he came hither, and the battles that he met with in this place, be a warning to those that come after." Lo, said their guide, did not I tell you that there was something hereabouts that would give intimation of the reason why Christian was so hard beset in this place? Then turning to Christiana, he said, No disparagement to Christian more than to any others whose hap and lot it was. For it is easier going up than down this hill, and that can be said but of few hills in all these parts of the world. But we will leave the good man; he is at rest: he also had a brave victory over his enemy. Let Him grant, that dwelleth above, that we fare no worse, when we come be tried, than he.

But we will come again to this Valley of Humiliation. It is the best and most fruitful piece of ground in all those parts. It is fat ground, and as you see, consisteth much in meadows; and if a man was to come here in the summer-time, as we do now, if he knew not anything before thereof, and if he also delighted himself in the sight of his eyes, he might see that which would be delightful to him. Behold how green this valley is; also how beautified with lilies. (Song 2:1). I have known many laboring men that have got good estates in this Valley of Humiliation; for God resisteth the proud, but giveth grace to the humble. (James 4:6; 1 Pet. 5:5). Indeed it is a very fruitful soil, and doth bring forth by handfuls. Some also have wished that the next way to their Father's house were here, that they might be troubled no more with either hills or mountains to go over; but the way is the way, and there is an end.

Now, as they were going along, and talking, they espied a boy feeding his father's sheep. The boy was in very mean clothes, but of a very fresh and well-favored countenance; and as he sat by himself, he sung. Hark, said Mr. Great-Heart, to what the shepherd's boy saith. So they hearkened and he said,

"He that is down, needs fear no fall;
He that is low, no pride:
He that is humble, ever shall
Have God to be his guide.

I am content with what I have,
Little be it or much;
And, Lord, contentment still I crave,
Because thou savest such.

Fullness to such, a burden is,
That go on pilgrimage;
Here little, and hereafter bliss,
Is best from Age to Age."

Then said the guide, Do you hear him? I will dare to say, that this boy lives a merrier life, and wears more of that herb called heart's-ease in his bosom, than he that is clad in silk and velvet. But we will proceed in our discourse.

In this valley our Lord formerly had his country-house: he loved much to be here. He loved also to walk these meadows, for he found the air was pleasant. Besides, here a man shall be free from the noise, and from the hurrying of this life: all states are full of noise and confusion; only the Valley of Humiliation is that empty and solitary place. Here a man shall not be so let and hindered in his contemplation as in other places he is apt to be. This is a valley that nobody walks in but those that love a pilgrim's life. And though Christian had the hard hap to meet here with Apollyon, and to enter with him in a brisk encounter, yet I must tell you, that in former times men have met with angels here, (Hos. 12:4,5), have found pearls here, (Matt. 13:46), and have in this place found the words of life. (Prov. 8:36).

Did I say our Lord had here in former days his country-house, and that he loved here to walk? I will add-in this place, and to the people that love and trace these grounds, he has left a yearly revenue, to be faithfully paid them at certain seasons, for their maintenance by the way, and for their further encouragement to go on in their pilgrimage.

Samuel: Now, as they went on, Samuel said to Mr. Great-Heart, Sir, I perceive that in this valley my father and Apollyon had their battle; but whereabout was the fight? for I perceive this valley is large.

Mr. Great-Heart: Your father had the battle with Apollyon at a place yonder before us, in a narrow passage, just beyond Forgetful Green. And indeed that place is the most dangerous place in all these parts. For if at any time pilgrims meet with any brunt, it is when they forget what favors they have received, and how unworthy they are of them. This is the place also where others have been hard put to it. But more of the place when we are come to it; for I persuade myself that to this day there remains either some sign of the battle, or some monument to testify that such a battle there was fought.

Mercy: Then said Mercy, I think I am as well in this valley as I have been anywhere else in all our journey: the place, methinks, suits with my spirit. I love to be in such places, where there is no rattling with coaches, nor rumbling with wheels. Methinks, here one may, without much molestation, be thinking what he is, whence he came, what he has done, and to what the King has called him. Here one may think, and break at heart, and melt in one's spirit, until one's eyes become as the fish-pools in Heshbon. (Song 7:4). They that go rightly through this valley of Baca, make it a well; the rain that God sends down from heaven upon them that are here, also filleth the pools. This valley is that from whence also the King will give to his their vineyards; and they that go through it shall sing, as Christian did, for all he met with Apollyon. (Ps. 84:5-7; Hos. 2:15).

Mr. Great-Heart: 'Tis true, said their guide; I have gone through this valley many a time, and never was better than when here. I have also been a conduct to several pilgrims, and they have confessed the same. "To this man will I look," saith the King, "even to him that is poor, and of a contrite spirit, and trembleth at my word." (Is. 66:2).

Now they were come to the place where the aforementioned battle was fought: Then said the guide to Christiana, her children, and Mercy, This is the place; on this ground Christian stood, and up there came Apollyon against him; and look. And, look, did I not tell you? here is some of your husband's blood upon these stones to this day: Behold, also, how here and there are yet to be seen upon the place, some of the shivers of Apollyon's broken darts. See, also, how they did beat the ground with their feet as they fought, to make good their places against each other; how also with their by-blows they did split the very stones in pieces. Verily, Christian did here play the man, and showed himself as stout as Hercules could, had he been there, even he himself. When Apollyon was beat, he made his retreat to the next valley, that is called, the Valley of the Shadow of Death, unto which we shall come anon. Lo, yonder also stands a monument, on which is engraved this battle, and Christian's victory, to his fame, throughout all ages: So because it stood just on the way-side before them, they stepped to it, and read the writing, which word for word was this:

"Hard by here was a battle fought,
Most strange, and yet most true;
Christian and Apollyon fought
Each other to subdue.

The man so bravely play'd the man,
He made the fiend to fly;
Of which a monument I stand,
The same to testify."

When they had passed by this place, they came upon the borders of the Shadow of Death. This Valley was longer than the other; a place also most strangely haunted with evil things, as many are able to testify: but these women and children went the better through it, because they had daylight, and because Mr. Great-Heart was their conductor.

When they were entering upon this valley, they thought they heard a groaning, as of dying men; a very great groaning. They thought also that they did hear words of lamentation, spoken as of some in extreme torment. These things made the boys to quake; the women also looked pale and wan; but their guide bid them be of good comfort.

So they went on a little further, and they thought that they felt the ground begin to shake under them, as if some hollow place was there: they heard also a kind of hissing, as of serpents, but nothing as yet appeared. Then said the boys, Are we not yet at the end of this doleful place? But the guide also bid them be of good courage, and look well to their feet; lest haply, said he, you be taken in some snare.

Now James began to be sick; but I think the cause thereof was fear: so his mother gave him some of that glass of spirits that had been given her at the Interpreter's house, and three of the pills that Mr. Skill had prepared, and the boy began to revive. Thus they went on till they came to about the middle of the valley; and then Christiana said, Methinks I see something yonder upon the road before us, a thing of a shape such as I have not seen. Then said Joseph, Mother, what is it? An ugly thing, child; an ugly thing, said she. But, mother, what is it like? said he. 'Tis like I cannot tell what, said she; and now it is but a little way off. Then said she, It is nigh.

Well, said Mr. Great-Heart, let them that are most afraid keep close to me. So the fiend came on, and the conductor met it; but when it was come to him, it vanished to all their sights. Then remembered they what had been said some time ago: "Resist the devil, and he will flee from you." (James 4:7).

They went therefore on, as being a little refreshed. But they had not gone far, before Mercy, looking behind her, saw, as she thought, something most like a lion, and it came at a great padding pace after: and it had a hollow voice of roaring; and at every roar it gave, it made the valley echo, and all their hearts to ache, save the heart of him that was their guide. So it came up and Mr. Great-Heart went behind, and put the pilgrims all before him. The lion also came on apace, and Mr. Great-Heart addressed himself to give him battle. (1 Pet. 5:8,9). But when he saw that it was determined that resistance should be made, he also drew back, and came no further.

Then they went on again, and their conductor went before them, till they came to a place where was cast up a pit the whole breadth of the way; and before they could be prepared to go over that, a great mist and a darkness fell upon them, so that they could not see. Then said the pilgrims, Alas! what now shall we do? But their guide made answer, Fear not; stand still, and see what an end will be put to this also; so they stayed there, because their path was marred. They then also thought that they did hear more apparently the noise and rushing of the enemies; the fire also and the smoke of the pit were much easier to be discerned. Then said Christiana to Mercy, Now I see what my poor husband went through. I have heard much of this place, but I never was here before now. Poor man! he went here all alone in the night; he had night almost quite through the way: also these fiends were busy about him, as if they would have torn him in pieces. Many have spoken of it; but none can tell what the Valley of the Shadow of Death should mean until they come in themselves. The heart knoweth its own bitterness; and a stranger intermeddleth not with its joy. (Pr. 14:10). To be here is a fearful thing.

Mr. Great-Heart: This is like doing business in great waters, or like going down into the deep. This is like being in the heart of the sea, and like going down to the bottoms of the mountains. Now it seems as if the earth, with its bars, were about us forever. But let them that walk in darkness, and have no light, trust in the name of the Lord, and stay upon their God. (Is. 50:10). For my part, as I have told you already, I have gone often through this valley, and have been much harder put to it than now I am: and yet you see I am alive. I would not boast, for that I am not mine own savior; but I trust we shall have a good deliverance. Come, let us pray for light to Him that can lighten our darkness, and that can rebuke not only these, but all the Satans in hell.

So they cried and prayed, and God sent light and deliverance, for there was now no let in their way; no, not there where but now they were stopped with a pit. Yet they were not got through the valley. So they went on still, and met with great stinks and loathsome smells, to the great annoyance of them. Then said Mercy to Christiana, It is not so pleasant being here as at the gate, or at the Interpreter's, or at the house where we lay last.

O but, said one of the boys, it is not so bad to go through here, as it is to abide here, always; and for aught I know, one reason why we must go this way to the house prepared for us is, that our home might be the sweeter to us.

Well said, Samuel, quoth the guide; thou hast now spoke like a man. Why, if ever I get out here again, said the boy, I think I shall prize light and good way better than I ever did in all my life. Then said the guide, We shall be out by and by.

So on they went, and Joseph said, Cannot we see to the end of this valley as yet? Then said the guide, Look to your feet, for we shall presently be among the snares: so they looked to their feet, and went on; but they were troubled much with the snares. Now, when they were come among the snares, they espied a man cast into the ditch on the left hand, with his flesh all rent and torn. Then said the guide, That is one Heedless, that was going this way: he has lain there a great while. There was one Take-Heed with him when he was taken and slain, but he escaped their hands. You cannot imagine how many are killed hereabouts, and yet men are so foolishly venturous as to set out lightly on pilgrimage, and to come without a guide. Poor Christian! it was a wonder that he here escaped; but he was beloved of his God: also he had a good heart of his own, or else he could never have done it.

Now they drew towards the end of this way; and just there where Christian had seen the cave when he went by, out thence came forth Maul, a giant. This Maul did use to spoil young pilgrims with sophistry; and he called Great-Heart by his name, and said unto him, How many times have you been forbidden to do these things? Then said Mr. Great-Heart, What things? What things! quoth the giant; you know what things: but I will put an end to your trade.

But, pray, said Mr. Great-Heart, before we fall to it, let us understand wherefore we must fight. Now the women and children stood trembling, and knew not what to do. Quoth the giant, You rob the country, and rob it with the worst of thefts. These are but generals, said Mr. Great-Heart; come to particulars, man.

Then said the giant, Thou practisest the craft of a kidnapper; thou gatherest up women and children, and carriest them into a strange country, to the weakening of my master's kingdom. But now Great-Heart replied, I am a servant of the God of heaven; my business is to persuade sinners to repentance. I am commanded to do my endeavors to turn men, women, and children, from darkness to light, and from the power of Satan unto God; and if this be indeed the ground of thy quarrel, let us fall to it as soon as thou wilt.

Then the giant came up, and Mr. Great-Heart went to meet him; and as he went he drew his sword, but the giant had a club. So without more ado they fell to it, and at the first blow the giant struck Mr. Great-Heart down upon one of his knees. With that the women and children cried out. So Mr. Great-Heart recovering himself, laid about him in full lusty manner, and gave the giant a wound in his arm. Thus he fought for the space of an hour, to that height of heat that the breath came out of the giant's nostrils as the heat doth out of a boiling cauldron.

Then they sat down to rest them; but Mr. Great-Heart betook himself to prayer. Also the women and children did nothing but sigh and cry all the time that the battle did last.

When they had rested them, and taken breath, they both fell to it again; and Mr. Great-Heart, with a blow, fetched the giant down to the ground. Nay, hold, let me recover, quoth he: so Mr. Great-Heart fairly let him get up. So to it they went again, and the giant missed but little of all to breaking Mr. Great-Heart's scull with his club.

Mr. Great-Heart seeing that, runs to him in the full heat of his spirit, and pierceth him under the fifth rib. With that the giant began to faint, and could hold up his club no longer. Then Mr. Great-Heart seconded his blow, and smit the head of the giant from his shoulders. Then the women and children rejoiced, and Mr. Great-Heart also praised God for the deliverance he had wrought.

When this was done, they amongst them erected a pillar, and fastened the giant's head thereon, and wrote under in letters that passengers might read,

"He that did wear this head was one
That pilgrims did misuse;
He stopped their way, he spared none,
But did them all abuse;
Until that I Great-Heart arose,
The pilgrims guide to be;
Until that I did him oppose
That was their enemy."

THE SIXTH STAGE

Now I saw that they went on to the ascent that was a little way off, cast up to be a prospect for pilgrims. That was the place from whence Christian had the first sight of Faithful his brother. Wherefore, here they sat down and rested. They also here did eat and drink, and make merry, for that they had gotten deliverance from this so dangerous an enemy. As they sat thus and did eat, Christiana asked the guide, if he had caught no hurt in the battle? Then said Mr. Great-Heart, No, save a little on my flesh; yet that also shall be so far from being to my detriment, that it is at present a proof of my love to my master and you, and shall be a means, by grace, to increase my reward at last.

Christiana: But were you not afraid, good sir, when you saw him come with his club?

Mr. Great-Heart: It is my duty, said he, to mistrust my own ability, that I may have reliance on Him who is stronger than all.

Christiana: But what did you think when he fetched you down to the ground at the first blow?

Mr. Great-Heart: Why, I thought, quoth he, that so my Master himself was served, and yet he it was that conquered at last. (2 Cor. 4:10,11; Rom. 8:37).

Matthew: When you all have thought what you please, I think God has been wonderfully good unto us, both in bringing us out of this valley, and in delivering us out of the hand of this enemy.

For my part, I see no reason why we should distrust our God any more, since he has now, and in such a place as this, given us such testimony of his love. Then they got up, and went forward.

Now a little before them stood an oak; and under it, when they came to it, they found an old pilgrim fast asleep. They knew that he was a pilgrim by his clothes, and his staff, and his girdle.

So the guide, Mr. Great-Heart, awaked him; and the old gentleman, as he lifted up his eyes, cried out, What's the matter? Who are you; and what is your business here?

Mr. Great-Heart: Come, man, be not so hot; here are none but friends. Yet the old man gets up, and stands upon his guard, and will know of them what they are. Then said the guide, My name is Great-Heart: I am the guide of these pilgrims that are going to the Celestial country.

Mr. Honest: Then said Mr. Honest, I cry you mercy: I feared that you had been of the company of those that some time ago did rob Little-Faith of his money; but, now I look better about me, I perceive you are honester people.

Mr. Great-Heart: Why, what would or could you have done to have helped yourself, if indeed we had been of that company?

Mr. Honest: Done! Why, I would have fought as long as breath had been in me: and had I so done, I am sure you could never have given me the worst on't; for a Christian can never be overcome, unless he shall yield of himself.

Mr. Great-Heart: Well said, father Honest, quoth the guide; for by this I know thou art a cock of the right kind, for thou hast said the truth.

Mr. Honest: And by this also I know that thou knowest what true pilgrimage is; for all others do think that we are the soonest overcome of any.

Mr. Great-Heart: Well, now we are so happily met, pray let me crave your name, and the name of the place you came from.

Mr. Honest: My name I cannot tell you, but I came from the town of Stupidity: it lieth about four degrees beyond the city of Destruction.

Mr. Great-Heart: Oh, Are you that countryman? Then I deem I have half a guess of you: your name is Old Honesty, is it not?

Mr. Honest: So the old gentleman blushed, and said, Not honesty in the abstract, but Honest is my name; and I wish that my nature may agree to what I am called. But, sir, said the old gentleman, how could you guess that I am such a man, since I came from such a place?

Mr. Great-Heart: I had heard of you before, by my Master; for he knows all things that are done on the earth. But I have often wondered that any should come from your place; for your town is worse than is the city of Destruction itself.

Mr. Honest: Yes, we lie more off from the sun, and so are more cold and senseless. But were a man in a mountain of ice, yet if the Sun of righteousness will arise upon him, his frozen heart shall feel a thaw; and thus it has been with me.

Mr. Great-Heart: I believe it, father Honest, I believe it; for I know the thing is true.

Then the old gentleman saluted all the pilgrims with a holy kiss of charity, and asked them their names, and how they had fared since they set out on their pilgrimage.

Christiana: Then said Christiana, My name I suppose you have heard of; good Christian was my husband, and these four are his children. But can you think how the old gentleman was taken, when she told him who she was? He skipped, he smiled, he blessed them with a thousand good wishes, saying:

Mr. Honest: I have heard much of your husband, and of his travels and wars which he underwent in his days. Be it spoken to your comfort, the name of your husband rings all over these parts of the world: his faith, his courage, his enduring, and his sincerity under all, had made his name famous. Then he turned him to the boys, and asked them of their names, which they told him. Then said he unto them, Matthew, be thou like Matthew the publican, not in vice, but in virtue. (Matt. 10:3). Samuel, said he, be thou like Samuel the prophet, a man of faith and prayer. (Ps. 99:6). Joseph, said he, be thou like Joseph in Potiphar's house, chaste, and one that flees from temptation. (Gen. 39). And James, be thou like James the just, and like James the brother of our Lord. (Acts 1:13). Then they told him of Mercy, and how she had left her town and her kindred to come along with Christiana and with her sons. At that the old honest man said, Mercy is thy name: by mercy shalt thou be sustained and carried through all those difficulties that shall assault thee in thy way, till thou shalt come thither where thou shalt look the Fountain of mercy in the face with comfort. All this while the guide, Mr. Great-Heart, was very well pleased, and smiled upon his companions.

Now, as they walked along together, the guide asked the old gentleman if he did not know one Mr. Fearing, that came on pilgrimage out of his parts.

Mr. Honest: Yes, very well, said he. He was a man that had the root of the matter in him; but he was one of the most troublesome pilgrims that ever I met with in all my days.

Mr. Great-Heart: I perceive you knew him, for you have given a very right character of him.

Mr. Honest: Knew him! I was a great companion of his; I was with him most an end; when he first began to think upon what would come upon us hereafter, I was with him.

Mr. Great-Heart: I was his guide from my Master's house to the gates of the Celestial City.

Mr. Honest: Then you knew him to be a troublesome one.

Mr. Great-Heart: I did so; but I could very well bear it; for men of my calling are oftentimes entrusted with the conduct of such as he was.

Mr. Honest: Well then, pray let us hear a little of him, and how he managed himself under your conduct.

Mr. Great-Heart: Why, he was always afraid that he should come short of whither he had a desire to go. Everything frightened him that he heard anybody speak of, if it had but the least appearance of opposition in it. I heard that he lay roaring at the Slough of Despond for above a month together; nor durst he, for all he saw several go over before him, venture, though they many of them offered to lend him their hands. He would not go back again, neither. The Celestial City-he said he should die if he came not to it; and yet he was dejected at every difficulty, and stumbled at every straw that any body cast in his way. Well, after he had lain at the Slough of Despond a great while, as I have told you, one sunshiny morning, I do not know how, he ventured, and so got over; but when he was over, he would scarce believe it. He had, I think, a Slough of Despond in his mind, a slough that he carried everywhere with him, or else he could never have been as he was. So he came up to the gate, you know what I mean, that stands at the head of this way, and there also he stood a good while before he would venture to knock. When the gate was opened, he would give back, and give place to others, and say that he was not worthy. For, all he got before some to the gate, yet many of them went in before him. There the poor man would stand shaking and shrinking; I dare say it would have pitied one's heart to have seen him. Nor would he go back again. At last he took the hammer that hanged on the gate, in his hand, and gave a small rap or two; then one opened to him, but he shrunk back as before. He that opened stepped out after him, and said, Thou trembling one, what wantest thou? With that he fell down to the ground. He that spoke to him wondered to see him so faint, so he said to him, Peace be to thee; up, for I have set open the door to thee; come in, for thou art blessed. With that he got up, and went in trembling; and when he was in, he was ashamed to show his face. Well, after he had been entertained there a while, as you know how the manner is, he was bid go on his way, and also told the way he should take. So he went on till he came out to our house; but as he behaved himself at the gate, so he did at my Master the Interpreter's door. He lay there about in the cold a good while, before he would adventure to call; yet he would not go back: and the nights were long and cold then. Nay, he had a note of necessity in his bosom to my master to receive him, and grant him the comfort of his house, and also to allow him a stout and valiant conductor, because he was himself so chicken-hearted a man; and yet for all that he was afraid to call at the door. So he lay up and down thereabouts, till, poor man, he was almost starved; yea, so great was his dejection, that though he saw several others for knocking get in, yet he was afraid to venture. At last, I think I looked out of the window, and perceiving a man to be up and down about the door, I went out to him, and asked what he was: but, poor man, the water stood in his eyes; so I perceived what he wanted. I went therefore in, and told it in the house, and we showed the thing to our Lord: so he sent me out again, to entreat him to come in; but I dare say, I had hard work to do it. At last he came in; and I will say that for my Lord, he carried it wonderful lovingly to him. There were but a few good bits at the table, but some of it was laid upon his trencher. Then he presented the note; and my Lord looked thereon, and said his desire should be granted. So when he had been there a good while, he seemed to get some heart, and to be a little more comfortable. For my Master, you must know, is one of very tender bowels, especially to them that are afraid; wherefore he carried it so towards him as might tend most to his encouragement. Well, when he had had a sight of the things of the place, and was ready to take his journey to go to the city, my Lord, as he did to Christian before, gave him a bottle of spirits, and some comfortable things to eat. Thus we set forward, and I went before him; but the man was but of few words, only he would sigh aloud.

When we were come to where the three fellows were hanged, he said that he doubted that that would be his end also. Only he seemed glad when he saw the cross and the sepulcher. There I confess he desired to stay a little to look; and he seemed for a while after to be a little cheery. When he came to the Hill Difficulty, he made no stick at that, nor did he much fear the lions: for you must know, that his troubles were not about such things as these; his fear was about his acceptance at last.

I got him in at the house Beautiful, I think, before he was willing. Also, when he was in, I brought him acquainted with the damsels of the place; but he was ashamed to make himself much in company. He desired much to be alone; yet he always loved good talk, and often would get behind the screen to hear it. He also loved much to see ancient things, and to be pondering them in his mind. He told me afterward, that he loved to be in those two houses from which he came last, to wit, at the gate, and that of the Interpreter, but that he durst not be so bold as to ask.

When we went also from the house Beautiful, down the hill, into the Valley of Humiliation, he went down as well as ever I saw a man in my life; for he cared not how mean he was, so he might be happy at last. Yea, I think there was a kind of sympathy betwixt that Valley and him; for I never saw him better in all his pilgrimage than he was in that Valley.

Here he would lie down, embrace the ground, and kiss the very flowers that grew in this valley. (Lam. 3:27-29). He would now be up every morning by break of day, tracing and walking to and fro in the valley.

But when he was come to the entrance of the Valley of the Shadow of Death, I thought I should have lost my man: not for that he had any inclination to go back; that he always abhorred; but he was ready to die for fear. Oh, the hobgoblins will have me! the hobgoblins will have me! cried he; and I could not beat him out of it. He made such a noise, and such an outcry here, that had they but heard him, it was enough to encourage them to come and fall upon us.

But this I took very great notice of, that this valley was as quiet when we went through it, as ever I knew it before or since. I suppose those enemies here had now a special check from our Lord, and a command not to meddle until Mr. Fearing had passed over it.

It would be too tedious to tell you of all; we will therefore only mention a passage or two more. When he was come to Vanity Fair, I thought he would have fought with all the men in the fair. I feared there we should have been both knocked on the head, so hot was he against their fooleries. Upon the Enchanted Ground he was very wakeful. But when he was come at the river where was no bridge, there again he was in a heavy case. Now, now, he said, he should be drowned forever, and so never see that face with comfort that he had come so many miles to behold.

And here also I took notice of what was very remarkable: the water of that river was lower at this time than ever I saw it in all my life; so he went over at last, not much above wetshod. When he was going up to the gate, I began to take leave of him, and to wish him a good reception above. So he said, I shall, I shall. Then parted we asunder, and I saw him no more.

Mr. Honest: Then it seems he was well at last?

Mr. Great-Heart: Yes, yes, I never had doubt about him. He was a man of a choice spirit, only he was always kept very low, and that made his life so burdensome to himself, and so troublesome to others. (Ps. 88). He was, above many, tender of sin: he was so afraid of doing injuries to others, that he often would deny himself of that which was lawful, because he would not offend. (Rom. 14:21; 1 Cor. 8:13).

Mr. Honest: But what should be the reason that such a good man should be all his days so much in the dark?

Mr. Great-Heart: There are two sorts of reasons for it. One is, the wise God will have it so: some must pipe, and some must weep. (Matt. 11:16). Now Mr. Fearing was one that played upon the bass. He and his fellows sound the sackbut, whose notes are more doleful than the notes of other music are: though indeed, some say, the bass is the ground of music. And for my part, I care not at all for that profession which begins not in heaviness of mind. The first string that the musician usually touches is the bass, when he intends to put all in tune. God also plays upon this string first, when he sets the soul in tune for himself. Only there was the imperfection of Mr. Fearing; he could play upon no other music but this till towards his latter end.

[I make bold to talk thus metaphorically for the ripening of the wits of young readers, and because, in the book of Revelation, the saved are compared to a company of musicians, that play upon their trumpets and harps, and sing their songs before the throne. (Rev. 5:8; 14:2, 3).]

Mr. Honest: He was a very zealous man, as one may see by the relation you have given of him. Difficulties, lions, or Vanity Fair, he feared not at all; it was only sin, death, and hell, that were to him a terror, because he had some doubts about his interest in that celestial country.

Mr. Great-Heart: You say right; those were the things that were his troublers; and they, as you have well observed, arose from the weakness of his mind thereabout, not from weakness of spirit as to the practical part of a pilgrim's life. I dare believe that, as the proverb is, he could have bit a firebrand, had it stood in his way; but the things with which he was oppressed, no man ever yet could shake off with ease.

Christiana: Then said Christiana, This relation of Mr. Fearing has done me good; I thought nobody had been like me. But I see there was some semblance betwixt this good man and me: only we differed in two things. His troubles were so great that they broke out; but mine I kept within. His also lay so hard upon him, they made him that he could not knock at the houses provided for entertainment; but my trouble was always such as made me knock the louder.

Mercy: If I might also speak my heart, I must say that something of him has also dwelt in me. For I have ever been more afraid of the lake, and the loss of a place in paradise, than I have been of the loss other things. O, thought I, may I have the happiness to have a habitation there! 'Tis enough, though I part with all the world to win it.

Matthew: Then said Matthew, Fear was one thing that made me think that I was far from having that within me which accompanies salvation. But if it was so with such a good man as he, why may it not also go well with me?

James: No fears no grace, said James. Though there is not always grace where there is the fear of hell, yet, to be sure, there is no grace where there is no fear of God.

Mr. Great-Heart: Well said, James; thou hast hit the mark. For the fear of God is the beginning of wisdom; and to be sure, they that want the beginning have neither middle nor end. But we will here conclude our discourse of Mr. Fearing, after we have sent after him this farewell.

"Well, Master Fearing, thou didst fear
Thy God, and wast afraid
Of doing anything, while here,
That would have thee betrayed.
And didst thou fear the lake and pit?
Would others do so too!
For, as for them that want thy wit,
They do themselves undo."

Now I saw that they still went on in their talk. For after Mr. Great-Heart had made an end with Mr. Fearing, Mr. Honest began to tell them of another, but his name was Mr. Self-will. He pretended himself to be a pilgrim, said Mr. Honest; but I persuade myself he never came in at the gate that stands at the head of the way.

Mr. Great-Heart: Had you ever any talk with him about it?

Mr. Honest: Yes, more than once or twice; but he would always be like himself, self-willed. He neither cared for man, nor argument, nor yet example; what his mind prompted him to, that he would do, and nothing else could he be got to do.

Mr. Great-Heart: Pray, what principles did he hold? for I suppose you can tell.

Mr. Honest: He held that a man might follow the vices as well as the virtues of pilgrims; and that if he did both, he should be certainly saved.

Mr. Great-Heart: How? If he had said, it is possible for the best to be guilty of the vices, as well as to partake of the virtues of pilgrims, he could not much have been blamed; for indeed we are exempted from no vice absolutely, but on condition that we watch and strive. But this, I perceive, is not the thing; but if I understand you right, your meaning is, that he was of opinion that it was allowable so to be.

Mr. Honest: Aye, aye, so I mean, and so he believed and practiced.

Mr. Great-Heart: But what grounds had he for his so saying?

Mr. Honest: Why, he said he had the Scripture for his warrant.

Mr. Great-Heart: Prithee, Mr. Honest, present us with a few particulars.

Mr. Honest: So I will. He said, to have to do with other men's wives had been practiced by David, God's beloved; and therefore he could do it. He said, to have more women than one was a thing that Solomon practiced, and therefore he could do it. He said, that Sarah and the godly midwives of Egypt lied, and so did save Rahab, and therefore he could do it. He said, that the disciples went at the bidding of their Master, and took away the owner's ass, and therefore he could do so too. He said, that Jacob got the inheritance of his father in a way of guile and dissimulation, and therefore he could do so too.

Mr. Great-Heart: High base indeed! And are you sure he was of this opinion?

Mr. Honest: I heard him plead for it, bring Scripture for it, bring arguments for it, etc.

Mr. Great-Heart: An opinion that is not fit to be with any allowance in the world!

Mr. Honest: You must understand me rightly: he did not say that any man might do this; but that they who had the virtues of those that did such things, might also do the same.

Mr. Great-Heart: But what more false than such a conclusion? For this is as much as to say, that because good men heretofore have sinned of infirmity, therefore he had allowance to do it of a presumptuous mind; or that if, because a child, by the blast of the wind, or for that it stumbled at a stone, fell down and defiled itself in the mire, therefore he might willfully lie down and wallow like a boar therein. Who could have thought that anyone could so far have been blinded by the power of lust? But what is written must be true: they "stumble at the word, being disobedient; whereunto also they were appointed." (1 Peter, 2:8). His supposing that such may have the godly men's virtues, who addict themselves to their vices, is also a delusion as strong as the other. To eat up the sin of God's people, (Hos. 4:8), as a dog licks up filth, is no sign that one is possessed with their virtues. Nor can I believe that one who is of this opinion, can at present have faith or love in him. But I know you have made strong objections against him; prithee what can he say for himself?

Mr. Honest: Why, he says, to do this by way of opinion, seems abundantly more honest than to do it, and yet hold contrary to it in opinion.

Mr. Great-Heart: A very wicked answer. For though to let loose the bridle to lusts, while our opinions are against such things, is bad; yet, to sin, and plead a toleration so to do, is worse: the one stumbles beholders accidentally, the other leads them into the snare.

Mr. Honest: There are many of this man's mind, that have not this man's mouth; and that makes going on pilgrimage of so little esteem as it is.

Mr. Great-Heart: You have said the truth, and it is to be lamented: but he that feareth the King of paradise, shall come out of them all.

Christiana: There are strange opinions in the world. I know one that said, it was time enough to repent when we come to die.

Mr. Great-Heart: Such are not overwise; that man would have been loth, might he have had a week to run twenty miles in his life, to defer his journey to the last hour of that week.

Mr. Honest: You say right; and yet the generality of them who count themselves pilgrims, do indeed do thus. I am, as you see, an old man, and have been a traveler in this road many a day; and I have taken notice of many things.

I have seen some that have set out as if they would drive all the world before them, who yet have, in a few days, died as they in the wilderness, and so never got sight of the promised land. I have seen some that have promised nothing at first setting out to be pilgrims, and who one would have thought could not have lived a day, that have yet proved very good pilgrims. I have seen some who have run hastily forward, that again have, after a little time, run just as fast back again. I have seen some who have spoken very well of a pilgrim's life at first, that after a while have spoken as much against it. I have heard some, when they first set out for paradise, say positively, there is such a place, who, when they have been almost there, have come back again, and said there is none. I have heard some vaunt what they would do in case they should be opposed, that have, even at a false alarm, fled faith, the pilgrim's way, and all.

Now, as they were thus on their way, there came one running to meet them, and said, Gentlemen, and you of the weaker sort, if you love life, shift for yourselves, for the robbers are before you.

Mr. Great-Heart: Then said Mr. Great-Heart, They be the three that set upon Little-Faith heretofore. Well, said he, we are ready for them: so they went on their way. Now they looked at every turning when they should have met with the villains; but whether they heard of Mr. Great-Heart, or whether they had some other game, they came not up to the pilgrims.

Christiana then wished for an inn to refresh herself and her children, because they were weary. Then said Mr. Honest, There is one a little before us, where a very honorable disciple, one Gaius, dwells. (Rom. 16:23). So they all concluded to turn in thither; and the rather, because the old gentleman gave him so good a report. When they came to the door they went in, not knocking, for folks use not to knock at the door of an inn. Then they called for the master of the house, and he came to them. So they asked if they might lie there that night.

Gaius: Yes, gentlemen, if you be true men; for my house is for none but pilgrims. Then were Christiana, Mercy, and the boys the more glad, for that the innkeeper was a lover of pilgrims. So they called for rooms, and he showed them one for Christiana and her children and Mercy, and another for Mr. Great-Heart and the old gentleman.

Mr. Great-Heart: Then said Mr. Great-Heart, good Gaius, what hast thou for supper? for these pilgrims have come far to-day, and are weary.

Gaius: It is late, said Gaius, so we cannot conveniently go out to seek food; but such as we have you shall be welcome to, if that will content.

Mr. Great-Heart: We will be content with what thou hast in the house; for as much as I have proved thee, thou art never destitute of that which is convenient.

Then he went down and spake to the cook, whose name was, Taste-that-which-is-good, to get ready supper for so many pilgrims. This done, he comes up again, saying, Come, my good friends, you are welcome to me, and I am glad that I have a house to entertain you in; and while supper is making ready, if you please, let us entertain one another with some good discourse: so they all said, Content.

Gaius: Then said Gaius, Whose wife is this aged matron? And whose daughter is this young damsel?

Mr. Great-Heart: This woman is the wife of one Christian, a pilgrim of former times; and these are his four children. The maid is one of her acquaintance, one that she hath persuaded to come with her on pilgrimage. The boys take all after their father, and covet to tread in his steps; yea, if they do but see any place where the old pilgrim hath lain, or any print of his foot, it ministereth joy to their hearts, and they covet to lie or tread in the same.

Gaius: Then said Gaius, Is this Christian's wife, and are these Christian's children? I knew your husband's father, yea, also his father's father. Many have been good of this stock; their ancestors dwelt first at Antioch. (Acts 11:26). Christian's progenitors (I suppose you have heard your husband talk of them) were very worthy men. They have, above any that I know, showed themselves men of great virtue and courage for the Lord of the pilgrims, his ways, and them that loved him. I have heard of many of your husband's relations that have stood all trials for the sake of the truth. Stephen, that was one of the first of the family from whence your husband sprang, was knocked on the head with stones. (Acts 7:59, 60). James, another of this generation, was slain with the edge of the sword. (Acts 12:2). To say nothing of Paul and Peter, men anciently of the family from whence your husband came, there was Ignatius, who was cast to the lions; Romanus, whose flesh was cut by pieces from his bones; and Polycarp, that played the man in the fire. There was he that was hanged up in a basket in the sun for the wasps to eat; and he whom they put into a sack, and cast him into the sea to be drowned. It would be impossible utterly to count up all of that family who have suffered injuries and death for the love of a pilgrim's life. Nor can I but be glad to see that thy husband has left behind him four such boys as these. I hope they will bear up their father's name, and tread in their father's steps, and come to their father's end.

Mr. Great-Heart: Indeed, sir, they are likely lads: they seem to choose heartily their father's ways.

Gaius: That is it that I said. Wherefore Christian's family is like still to spread abroad upon the face of the ground, and yet to be numerous upon the face of the earth; let Christiana look out some damsels for her sons, to whom they may be betrothed, etc., that the name of their father, and the house of his progenitors, may never be forgotten in the world.

Mr. Honest: 'Tis pity his family should fall and be extinct.

Gaius: Fall it cannot, but be diminished it may; but let Christiana take my advice, and that is the way to uphold it. And, Christiana, said this innkeeper, I am glad to see thee and thy friend Mercy together here, a lovely couple. And if I may advise, take Mercy into a nearer relation to thee: if she will, let her be given to Matthew thy eldest son. It is the way to preserve a posterity in the earth. So this match was concluded, and in process of time they were married: but more of that hereafter.

Gaius also proceeded, and said, I will now speak on the behalf of women, to take away their reproach. For as death and the curse came into the world by a woman, (Gen. 3), so also did life and health: God sent forth his Son, made of a woman. (Gal. 4:4). Yea, to show how much they that came after did abhor the act of the mother, this sex in the Old Testament coveted children, if happily this or that woman might be the mother of the Savior of the world. I will say again, that when the Savior was come, women rejoiced in him, before either man or angel. (Luke 1:42-46). I read not that ever any man did give unto Christ so much as one groat; but the women followed him, and ministered to him of their substance. (Luke 8:2, 3). 'Twas a woman that washed his feet with tears, (Luke 7:37-50), and a woman that anointed his body at the burial. (John 11:2; 12:3). They were women who wept when he was going to the cross, (Luke 23:27), and women that followed him from the cross, (Matt. 27:55,56; Luke 23:55), and sat over against his sepulcher when he was buried. (Matt. 27:61). They were women that were first with him at his resurrection-morn, (Luke 24:1), and women that brought tidings first to his disciples that he was risen from the dead. (Luke 24:22, 23). Women therefore are highly favored, and show by these things that they are sharers with us in the grace of life.

Now the cook sent up to signify that supper was almost ready, and sent one to lay the cloth, and the trenchers, and to set the salt and bread in order.

Then said Matthew, The sight of this cloth, and of this forerunner of the supper, begetteth in me a greater appetite for my food than I had before.

Gaius: So let all ministering doctrines to thee in this life beget in thee a greater desire to sit at the supper of the great King in his kingdom; for all preaching, books, and ordinances here, are but as the laying of the trenchers, and the setting of salt upon the board, when compared with the feast which our Lord will make for us when we come to his house.

So supper came up. And first a heave-shoulder and a wave-breast were set on the table before them; to show that they must begin their meal with prayer and praise to God. The heave-shoulder David lifted up his heart to God with; and with the wave-breast, where his heart lay, he used to lean upon his harp when he played. (Lev. 7: 32-34; 10:14,15; Ps. 25:1; Heb. 13:15). These two dishes were very fresh and good, and they all ate heartily thereof.

The next they brought up was a bottle of wine, as red as blood. (Deut. 32:14; Judges 9:13; John 15:5). So Gaius said to them, Drink freely; this is the true juice of the vine, that makes glad the heart of God and man. So they drank and were merry.

The next was a dish of milk well crumbed; Gaius said, Let the boys have that, that they may grow thereby. (1 Pet. 2:1,2).

Then they brought up in course a dish of butter and honey. Then said Gaius, Eat freely of this, for this is good to cheer up and strengthen your judgments and understandings. This was our Lord's dish when he was a child: "Butter and honey shall he eat, that he may know to refuse the evil, and choose the good." (Is. 7:15).

Then they brought them up a dish of apples, and they were very good-tasted fruit. Then said Matthew, May we eat apples, since it was such by and with which the serpent beguiled our first mother?

Then said Gaius:

"Apples were they with which we were beguil'd,
Yet sin, not apples, hath our souls defil'd:
Apples forbid, if ate, corrupt the blood;
To eat such, when commanded, does us good:
Drink of his flagons then, thou church, his dove,
And eat his apples, who art sick of love."

Then said Matthew, I made the scruple, because I a while since was sick with the eating of fruit.

Gaius: Forbidden fruit will make you sick; but not what our Lord has tolerated.

While they were thus talking, they were presented with another dish, and it was a dish of nuts. (Song 6:11). Then said some at the table, Nuts spoil tender teeth, especially the teeth of children: which when Gaius heard, he said:

"Hard texts are nuts, (I will not call them cheaters,)
Whose shells do keep the kernel from the eaters:
Open the shells, and you shall have the meat;
They here are brought for you to crack and eat."

Then were they very merry, and sat at the table a long time, talking of many things. Then said the old gentleman, My good landlord, while we are cracking your nuts, if you please, do you open this riddle:

"A man there was, though some did count him mad,
The more he cast away, the more he had."

Then they all gave good heed, wondering what good Gaius would say; so he sat still a while, and then thus replied:

"He who bestows his goods upon the poor,
Shall have as much again, and ten times more."

Then said Joseph, I dare say, sir, I did not think you could have found it out.

Oh, said Gaius, I have been trained up in this way a great while: nothing teaches like experience. I have learned of my Lord to be kind, and have found by experience that I have gained thereby. There is that scattereth, and yet increaseth; and there is that withholdeth more than is meet, but it tendeth to poverty: There is that maketh himself rich, yet hath nothing; there is that maketh himself poor, yet hath great riches. (Prov. 11:24; 13:7).

Then Samuel whispered to Christiana, his mother, and said, Mother, this is a very good man's house: let us stay here a good while, and let my brother Matthew be married here to Mercy, before we go any further. The which Gaius the host overhearing, said, With a very good will, my child.

So they stayed there more than a month, and Mercy was given to Matthew to wife.

While they stayed here, Mercy, as her custom was, would be making coats and garments to give to the poor, by which she brought a very good report upon the pilgrims.

But to return again to our story: After supper the lads desired a bed, for they were weary with travelling: Then Gaius called to show them their chamber; but said Mercy, I will have them to bed. So she had them to bed, and they slept well: but the rest sat up all night; for Gaius and they were such suitable company, that they could not tell how to part. After much talk of their Lord, themselves, and their journey, old Mr. Honest, he that put forth the riddle to Gaius, began to nod. Then said Great-Heart, What, sir, you begin to be drowsy; come, rub up, now here is a riddle for you. Then said Mr. Honest, Let us hear it. Then replied Mr. Great-heart,

"He that would kill, must first be overcome:
Who live abroad would, first must die at home."

Ha, said Mr. Honest, it is a hard one; hard to expound, and harder to practice. But come, landlord, said he, I will, if you please, leave my part to you: do you expound it, and I will hear what you say.

No, said Gaius, it was put to you, and it is expected you should answer it. Then said the old gentleman:

"He first by grace must conquered be,
That sin would mortify;
Who that he lives would convince me,
Unto himself must die."

It is right, said Gaius; good doctrine and experience teach this. For, first, until grace displays itself, and overcomes the soul with its glory, it is altogether without heart to oppose sin. Besides, if sin is Satan's cords, by which the soul lies bound, how should it make resistance before it is loosed from that infirmity? Secondly, Nor will any one that knows either reason or grace, believe that such a man can be a living monument of grace that is a slave to his own corruptions. And now it comes into my mind, I will tell you a story worth the hearing. There were two men that went on pilgrimage; the one began when he was young, the other when he was old. The young man had strong corruptions to grapple with; the old man's were weak with the decays of nature. The young man trod his steps as even as did the old one, and was every way as light as he. Who now, or which of them, had their graces shining clearest, since both seemed to be alike?

Mr. Honest: The young man's, doubtless. For that which makes head against the greatest opposition, gives best demonstration that it is strongest; especially when it also holdeth pace with that which meets not with half so much, as to be sure old age does not. Besides, I have observed that old men have blessed themselves with this mistake; namely, taking the decays of nature for a gracious conquest over corruptions, and so have been apt to beguile themselves.

Indeed, old men that are gracious are best able to give advice to them that are young, because they have seen most of the emptiness of things: but yet, for an old and a young man to set out both together, the young one has the advantage of the fairest discovery of a work of grace within him, though the old man's corruptions are naturally the weakest. Thus they sat talking till break of day.

Now, when the family were up, Christiana bid her son James that he should read a chapter; so he read Isaiah chapter 53. When he had done, Mr. Honest asked why it was said that the Savior was to come "out of a dry ground;" and also, that "he had no form nor comeliness in him."

Mr. Great-Heart: Then said Mr. Great-Heart: To the first I answer, because the church of the Jews, of which Christ came, had then lost almost all the sap and spirit of religion. To the second I say, the words are spoken in the person of unbelievers, who, because they want the eye that can see into our Prince's heart, therefore they judge of him by the meanness of his outside; just like those who, not knowing that precious stones are covered over with a homely crust, when they have found one, because they know not what they have found, cast it away again, as men do a common stone.

Well, said Gaius, now you are here, and since, as I know, Mr. Great-Heart is good at his weapons, if you please, after we have refreshed ourselves, we will walk into the fields, to see if we can do any good. About a mile from hence there is one Slay-good, a giant, that doth much annoy the King's highway in these parts; and I know whereabout his haunt is. He is master of a number of thieves: t would be well if we could clear these parts of him. So they consented and went: Mr. Great-Heart with his sword, helmet, and shield; and the rest with spears and staves.

When they came to the place where he was, they found him with one Feeble-mind in his hand, whom his servants had brought unto him, having taken him in the way. Now the giant was rifling him, with a purpose after that to pick his bones; for he was of the nature of flesh eaters.

Well, so soon as he saw Mr. Great-Heart and his friends at the mouth of his cave, with their weapons, he demanded what they wanted.

Mr. Great-Heart: We want thee; for we are come to revenge the quarrels of the many that thou hast slain of the pilgrims, when thou hast dragged them out of the King's highway: wherefore come out of thy cave. So he armed himself and came out, and to battle they went, and fought for above an hour, and then stood still to take wind.

Slay-Good: Then said the giant, Why are you here on my ground?

Mr. Great-Heart: To revenge the blood of pilgrims, as I told thee before. So they went to it again, and the giant made Mr. Great-Heart give back; but he came up again, and in the greatness of his mind he let fly with such stoutness at the giant's head and sides, that he made him let his weapon fall out of his hand. So he smote him, and slew him, and cut off his head, and brought it away to the inn. He also took Feeble-mind the pilgrim, and brought him with him to his lodgings. When they were come home, they showed his head to the family, and set it up, as they had done others before, for a terror to those that should attempt to do as he hereafter.

Then they asked Mr. Feeble-Mind how he fell into his hands. Mr. Feeble-Mind: Then said the poor man, I am a sickly man, as you see: and because death did usually once a day knock at my door,

I thought I should never be well at home; so I betook myself to a pilgrim's life, and have traveled hither from the town of Uncertain, where I and my father were born. I am a man of no strength at all of body, nor yet of mind, but would, if I could, though I can but crawl, spend my life in the pilgrim's way. When I came at the gate that is at the head of the way, the Lord of that place did entertain me freely; neither objected he against my weakly looks, nor against my feeble mind; but gave me such things as were necessary for my journey, and bid me hope to the end. When I came to the house of the Interpreter, I received much kindness there: and because the hill of Difficulty was judged too hard for me, I was carried up that by one of his servants. Indeed, I have found much relief from pilgrims, though none were willing to go so softly as I am forced to do: yet still as they came on, they bid me be of good cheer, and said, that it was the will of their Lord that comfort should be given to the feeble-minded, (1 Thess. 5:14); and so went on their own pace. When I was come to Assault-lane, then this giant met with me, and bid me prepare for an encounter. But, alas, feeble one that I was, I had more need of a cordial; so he came up and took me. I conceited he would not kill me. Also when he had got me into his den, since I went not with him willingly, I believed I should come out alive again; for I have heard, that not any pilgrim that is taken captive by violent hands, if he keeps heart whole towards his Master, is, by the laws of providence, to die by the hand of the enemy. Robbed I looked to be, and robbed to be sure I am; but I have, as you see, escaped with life, for the which I thank my King as the author, and you as the means. Other brunts I also look for; but this I have resolved on, to wit, to run when I can, to go when I cannot run, and to creep when I cannot go. As to the main, I thank him that loved me, I am fixed; my way is before me, my mind is beyond the river that has no bridge, though I am, as you see, but of a feeble mind.

Mr. Honest: Then said old Mr. Honest, Have not you, sometime ago, been acquainted with one Mr. Fearing, a pilgrim?

Mr. Feeble-Mind: Acquainted with him! Yes, he came from the town of Stupidity, which lieth four degrees to the northward of the city of Destruction, and as many off of where I was born: yet we were well acquainted, for indeed he was my uncle, my father's brother. He and I have been much of a temper: he was a little shorter than I, but yet we were much of a complexion.

Mr. Honest: I perceive you knew him, and I am apt to believe also that you were related one to another; for you have his whitely look, a cast like his with your eye, and your speech is much alike.

Mr. Feeble-Mind: Most have said so that have known us both: and, besides, what I have read in him I have for the most part found in myself.

Gaius: Come, sir, said good Gaius, be of good cheer; you are welcome to me, and to my house. What thou hast a mind to, call for freely; and what thou wouldst have my servants do for thee, they will do it with a ready mind.

Then said Mr. Feeble-mind, This is an unexpected favor, and as the sun shining out of a very dark cloud. Did giant Slay-good intend me this favor when he stopped me, and resolved to let me go no further? Did he intend, that after he had rifled my pockets I should go to Gaius mine host? Yet so it is.

Now, just as Mr. Feeble-mind and Gaius were thus in talk, there came one running, and called at the door, and said, that about a mile and a half off there was one Mr. Not-right, a pilgrim, struck dead upon the place where he was, with a thunderbolt.

Mr. Feeble-Mind: Alas! said Mr. Feeble-mind, is he slain? He overtook me some days before I came so far as hither, and would be my company-keeper. He was also with me when Slay-good the giant took me, but he was nimble of his heels, and escaped; but it seems he escaped to die, and I was taken to live.

"What one would think doth seek to slay outright,
Ofttimes delivers from the saddest plight.
That very Providence whose face is death,
Doth ofttimes to the lowly life bequeath.
I taken was, he did escape and flee;
Hands cross'd gave death to him and life to me."

Now, about this time Matthew and Mercy were married; also Gaius gave his daughter Phoebe to James, Matthew's brother, to wife; after which time they yet stayed about ten days at Gaius' house, spending their time and the seasons like as pilgrims use to do.

When they were to depart, Gaius made them a feast, and they did eat and drink, and were merry. Now the hour was come that they must be gone; wherefore Mr. Great-heart called for a reckoning. But Gaius told him, that at his house it was not the custom for pilgrims to pay for their entertainment. He boarded them by the year, but looked for his pay from the good Samaritan, who had promised him, at his return, whatsoever charge he was at with them, faithfully to repay him. (Luke 10:34,35). Then said Mr. Great-heart to him:

Mr. Great-Heart: Beloved, thou doest faithfully whatsoever thou doest to the brethren, and to strangers, who have borne witness of thy charity before the church, whom if thou yet bring forward on their journey, after a godly sort, thou shalt do well. (3 John 5,6). Then Gaius took his leave of them all, and his children, and particularly of Mr. Feeble-mind. He also gave him something to drink by the way.

Now Mr. Feeble-mind, when they were going out of the door, made as if he intended to linger. The which, when Mr. Great-Heart espied, he said, Come, Mr. Feeble-mind, pray do you go along with us: I will be your conductor, and you shall fare as the rest.

Mr. Feeble-Mind: Alas! I want a suitable companion. You are all lusty and strong, but I, as you see, am weak; I choose, therefore, rather to come behind, lest, by reason of my many infirmities, I should be both a burden to myself and to you. I am, as I said, a man of a weak and feeble mind, and shall be offended and made weak at that which others can bear. I shall like no laughing; I shall like no gay attire; I shall like no unprofitable questions. Nay, I am so weak a man as to be offended with that which others have a liberty to do. I do not yet know all the truth: I am a very ignorant Christian man. Sometimes, if I hear some rejoice in the Lord, it troubles me because I cannot do so too. It is with me as it is with a weak man among the strong, or as with a sick man among the healthy, or as a lamp despised; so that I know not what to do. "He that is ready to slip with his feet is as a lamp despised in the thought of him that is at ease." (Job 12:5).

Mr. Great-Heart: But, brother, said Mr. Great-Heart, I have it in commission to comfort the feeble-minded, and to support the weak. You must go along with us; we will wait for you; we will lend you our help; we will deny ourselves of some things, both opinionative and practical, for your sake: we will not enter into doubtful disputations before you; we will be made all things to you, rather than you shall be left behind. (1 Thess. 5:14; Rom. 14; 1 Cor. 8:9-13; 9:22).

Now, all this while they were at Gaius' door; and behold, as they were thus in the heat of their discourse, Mr. Ready-to-halt came by, with his crutches in his hand, and he also was going on pilgrimage.

Mr. Feeble-Mind: Then said Mr. Feeble-mind to him, Man, how camest thou hither? I was but now complaining that I had not a suitable companion, but thou art according to my wish. Welcome, welcome, good Mr. Ready-to-halt; I hope thou and I may be some help.

Mr. Ready-to-Halt: I shall be glad of thy company, said the other; and, good Mr. Feeble-mind, rather than we will part, since we are thus happily met, I will lend thee one of my crutches.

Mr. Feeble-Mind: Nay, said he, though I thank thee for thy good-will, I am not inclined to halt before I am lame. Howbeit, I think when occasion is, it may help me against a dog.

Mr. Ready-to-Halt: If either myself or my crutches can do thee a pleasure, we are both at thy command, good Mr. Feeble-mind.

Thus, therefore, they went on. Mr. Great-Heart and Mr. Honest went before, Christiana and her children went next, and Mr. Feeble-mind came behind, and Mr. Ready-to-halt with his crutches. Then said Mr. Honest:

Mr. Honest: Pray, sir, now we are upon the road, tell us some profitable things of some that have gone on pilgrimage before us.

Mr. Great-Heart: With a good will. I suppose you have heard how Christian of old did meet with Apollyon in the Valley of Humiliation, and also what hard work he had to go through the Valley of the Shadow of Death. Also I think you cannot but have heard how Faithful was put to it by Madam Wanton, with Adam the First, with one Discontent, and Shame; four as deceitful villains as a man can meet with upon the road.

Mr. Honest: Yes, I have heard of all this; but indeed good Faithful was hardest put to it with Shame: he was an unwearied one.

Mr. Great-Heart: Aye; for, as the pilgrim well said, he of all men had the wrong name.

Mr. Honest: But pray, sir, where was it that Christian and Faithful met Talkative? That same was also a notable one.

Mr. Great-Heart: He was a confident fool; yet many follow his ways.

Mr. Honest: He had like to have beguiled Faithful.

Mr. Great-Heart: Aye, but Christian put him into a way quickly to find him out.

Thus they went on till they came to the place where Evangelist met with Christian and Faithful, and prophesied to them what should befall them at Vanity Fair. Then said their guide, Hereabouts did Christian and Faithful meet with Evangelist, who prophesied to them of what troubles they should meet with at Vanity Fair.

Mr. Honest: Say you so? I dare say it was a hard chapter that then he did read unto them.

Mr. Great-Heart: It was so, but he gave them encouragement withal. But what do we talk of them? They were a couple of lion-like men; they had set their faces like a flint. Do not you remember how undaunted they were when they stood before the judge?

Mr. Honest: Well: Faithful bravely suffered.

Mr. Great-Heart: So he did, and as brave things came on't; for Hopeful, and some others, as the story relates it, were converted by his death.

Mr. Honest: Well, but pray go on; for you are well acquainted with things.

Mr. Great-Heart: Above all that Christian met with after he had passed through Vanity Fair, one By-ends was the arch one.

Mr. Honest: By-ends! what was he?

Mr. Great-Heart: A very arch fellow, a downright hypocrite; one that would be religious, whichever way the world went; but so cunning, that he would be sure never to lose or suffer for it. He had his mode of religion for every fresh occasion, and his wife was as good at it as he. He would turn from opinion to opinion; yea, and plead for so doing, too. But, so far as I could learn, he came to an ill end with his by-ends; nor did I ever hear that any of his children were ever of any esteem with any that truly feared God.

Now by this time they were come within sight of the town of Vanity, where Vanity Fair is kept. So, when they saw that they were so near the town, they consulted with one another how they should pass through the town; and some said one thing, and some another. At last Mr. Great-Heart said, I have, as you may understand, often been a conductor of pilgrims through this town. Now, I am acquainted with one Mr. Mnason, (Acts 21:16), of Cyprus, an old disciple, at whose house we may lodge. If you think good, we will turn in there.

Content, said old Honest; Content, said Christiana; Content, said Mr. Feeble-mind; and so they said all. Now you must think it was eventide by that they got to the outside of the town; but Mr. Great-Heart knew the way to the old man's house. So thither they came; and he called at the door, and the old man within knew his tongue as soon as ever he heard it; so he opened the door, and they all came in. Then said Mnason, their host, How far have ye come to-day? So they said, from the house of Gaius our friend. I promise you, said he, you have gone a good stitch. You may well be weary; sit down. So they sat down.

Mr. Great-Heart: Then said their guide, Come, what cheer, good sirs? I dare say you are welcome to my friend.

Mr. Mnason: I also, said Mr. Mnason, do bid you welcome; and whatever you want, do but say, and we will do what we can to get it for you.

Mr. Honest: Our great want, a while since, was harbor and good company, and now I hope we have both.

Mr. Mnason: For harbor, you see what it is; but for good company, that will appear in the trial.

Mr. Great-Heart: Well, said Mr. Great-Heart, will you have the pilgrims up into their lodging?

Mr. Mnason: I will, said Mr. Mnason So he had them to their respective places; and also showed them a very fair dining-room, where they might be, and sup together until the time should come to go to rest.

Now, when they were seated in their places, and were a little cheery after their journey, Mr. Honest asked his landlord if there was any store of good people in the town.

Mr. Mnason: We have a few: for indeed they are but a few when compared with them on the other side.

Mr. Honest: But how shall we do to see some of them? for the sight of good men to them that are going on pilgrimage, is like the appearing of the moon and stars to them that are sailing upon the seas.

Mr. Mnason: Then Mr. Mnason stamped with his foot, and his daughter Grace came up. So he said unto her, Grace, go you, tell my friends, Mr. Contrite, Mr. Holy-man, Mr. Love-saints, Mr. Dare-not-lie, and Mr. Penitent, that I have a friend or two at my house who have a mind this evening to see them. So Grace went to call them, and they came; and after salutation made, they sat down together at the table.

Then said Mr. Mnason their landlord, My neighbors, I have, as you see, a company of strangers come to my house; they are pilgrims: they come from afar, and are going to Mount Zion. But who, quoth he, do you think this is? pointing his finger to Christiana. It is Christiana, the wife of Christian, the famous pilgrim, who, with Faithful his brother, was so shamefully handled in our town. At that they stood amazed, saying, We little thought to see Christiana when Grace came to call us; wherefore this is a very comfortable surprise. They then asked her of her welfare, and if these young men were her husband's sons. And when she had told them they were, they said, The King whom you love and serve make you as your father, and bring you where he is in peace.

Mr. Honest: Then Mr. Honest (when they were all sat down) asked Mr. Contrite and the rest, in what posture their town was at present.

Mr. Contrite: You may be sure we are full of hurry in fair-time. T is hard keeping our hearts and spirits in good order when we are in a cumbered condition. He that lives in such a place as this is, and has to do with such as we have, has need of an item to caution him to take heed every moment of the day.

Mr. Honest: But how are your neighbors now for quietness?

Mr. Contrite: They are much more moderate now than formerly. You know how Christian and Faithful were used at our town; but of late, I say, they have been far more moderate. I think the blood of Faithful lieth as a load upon them till now; for since they burned him, they have been ashamed to burn any more. In those days we were afraid to walk the street; but now we can show our heads. Then the name of a professor was odious; now, especially in some parts of our town, (for you know our town is large,) religion is counted honorable. Then said Mr. Contrite to them, Pray how fareth it with you in your pilgrimage? how stands the country affected towards you?

Mr. Honest: It happens to us as it happeneth to wayfaring men: sometimes our way is clean, sometimes foul; sometimes up hill, sometimes down hill; we are seldom at a certainty. The wind is not always on our backs, nor is everyone a friend that we meet with in the way. We have met with some notable rubs already, and what are yet behind we know not; but for the most part, we find it true that has been talked of old, A good man must suffer trouble.

Mr. Contrite: You talk of rubs; what rubs have you met withal?

Mr. Honest: Nay, ask Mr. Great-Heart, our guide; for he can give the best account of that.

Mr. Great-Heart: We have been beset three or four times already. First, Christiana and her children were beset by two ruffians, who they feared would take away their lives. We were beset by Giant Bloody-man, Giant Maul, and Giant Slay-good. Indeed, we did rather beset the last than were beset by him. And thus it was: after we had been some time at the house of Gaius mine host, and of the whole church, we were minded upon a time to take our weapons with us, and go see if we could light upon any of those that are enemies to pilgrims; for we heard that there was a notable one thereabouts. Now Gaius knew his haunt better than I, because he dwelt thereabout. So we looked, and looked, till at last we discerned the mouth of his cave: then we were glad, and plucked up our spirits. So we approached up to his den; and lo, when we came there, he had dragged, by mere force, into his net, this poor man, Mr. Feeble-mind, and was about to bring him to his end. But when he saw us, supposing, as we thought, he had another prey, he left the poor man in his hole, and came out. So we fell to it full sore, and he lustily laid about him; but, in conclusion, he was brought down to the ground, and his head cut off, and set up by the way-side for a terror to such as should after practice such ungodliness. That I tell you the truth, here is the man himself to affirm it, who was as a lamb taken out of the mouth of the lion.

Mr. Feeble-Mind: Then said Mr. Feeble-mind, I found this true, to my cost and comfort: to my cost, when he threatened to pick my bones every moment; and to my comfort, when I saw Mr. Great-Heart and his friends, with their weapons, approach so near for my deliverance.

Mr. Holy-Man: Then said Mr. Holy-man, There are two things that they have need to possess who go on pilgrimage; courage, and an unspotted life. If they have not courage, they can never hold on their way; and if their lives be loose, they will make the very name of a pilgrim stink.

Mr. Love-Saints: Then said Mr. Love-saints, I hope this caution is not needful among you: but truly there are many that go upon the road, who rather declare themselves strangers to pilgrimage, than strangers and pilgrims on the earth.

Mr. Dare-Not-Lie: Then said Mr. Dare-not-lie, 'Tis true. They have neither the pilgrim's weed, nor the pilgrim's courage; they go not uprightly, but all awry with their feet; one shoe goeth inward, another outward; and their hosen are out behind: here a rag, and there a rent, to the disparagement of their Lord.

Mr. Penitent: These things, said Mr. Penitent, they ought to be troubled for; nor are the pilgrims like to have that grace put upon them and their Pilgrim's Progress as they desire, until the way is cleared of such spots and blemishes. Thus they sat talking and spending the time until supper was set upon the table, unto which they went, and refreshed their weary bodies: so they went to rest.

Now they staid in the fair a great while, at the house of Mr. Mnason, who in process of time gave his daughter Grace unto Samuel, Christian's son, to wife, and his daughter Martha to Joseph.

The time, as I said, that they staid here, was long, for it was not now as in former times. Wherefore the pilgrims grew acquainted with many of the good people of the town, and did them what service they could. Mercy, as she was wont, labored much for the poor: wherefore their bellies and backs blessed her, and she was there an ornament to her profession. And, to say the truth for Grace, Phebe, and Martha, they were all of a very good nature, and did much good in their places. They were also all of them very fruitful; so that Christian's name, as was said before, was like to live in the world.

While they lay here, there came a monster out of the woods, and slew many of the people of the town. It would also carry away their children, and teach them to suck its whelps. Now, no man in the town durst so much as face this monster; but all fled when they heard the noise of his coming.

The monster was like unto no one beast on the earth. Its body was like a dragon, and it had seven heads and ten horns. It made great havoc of children, and yet it was governed by a woman. (Rev. 17:3). This monster propounded conditions to men; and such men as loved their lives more than their souls, accepted of those conditions. So they came under.

Now Mr. Great-Heart, together with those who came to visit the pilgrims at Mr. Mnason's house, entered into a covenant to go and engage this beast, if perhaps they might deliver the people of this town from the paws and mouth of this so devouring a serpent. Then did Mr. Great-Heart, Mr. Contrite, Mr. Holy-man, Mr. Dare-not-lie, and Mr. Penitent, with their weapons, go forth to meet him. Now the monster at first was very rampant, and looked upon these enemies with great disdain; but they so belabored him, being sturdy men at arms, that they made him make a retreat: so they came home to Mr. Mnason's house again.

The monster, you must know, had his certain seasons to come out in, and to make his attempts upon the children of the people of the town. At these seasons did these valiant worthies watch him, and did still continually assault him; insomuch that in process of time he became not only wounded, but lame. Also he has not made that havoc of the townsmen's children as formerly he had done; and it is verily believed by some that this beast will die of his wounds.

This, therefore, made Mr. Great-Heart and his fellows of great fame in this town; so that many of the people that wanted their taste of things, yet had a reverent esteem and respect for them. Upon this account, therefore, it was, that these pilgrims got not much hurt here. True, there were some of the baser sort, that could see no more than a mole, nor understand any more than a beast; these had no reverence for these men, and took no notice of their valor and adventures.

THE SEVENTH STAGE

Well, the time grew on that the pilgrims must go on their way; wherefore they prepared for their journey. They sent for their friends; they conferred with them; they had some time set apart therein to commit each other to the protection of their Prince. There were again that brought them of such things as they had, that were fit for the weak and the strong, for the women and the men, and so laded them with such things as were necessary. (Acts 28:10). Then they set forward on their way; and their friends accompanying them so far as was convenient, they again committed each other to the protection of their King, and parted.

They therefore that were of the pilgrims' company went on, and Mr. Great-Heart went before them. Now, the women and children being weakly, they were forced to go as they could bear; by which means Mr. Ready-to-halt and Mr. Feeble-mind, had more to sympathize with their condition.

When they were gone from the townsmen, and when their friends had bid them farewell, they quickly came to the place where Faithful was put to death. Therefore they made a stand, and thanked him that had enabled him to bear his cross so well; and the rather, because they now found that they had a benefit by such a manly suffering as his was.

They went on therefore after this a good way further, talking of Christian and Faithful, and how Hopeful joined himself to Christian after that Faithful was dead.

Now they were come up with the hill Lucre, where the silver mine was which took Demas off from his pilgrimage, and into which, as some think, By-ends fell and perished; wherefore they considered that. But when they were come to the old monument that stood over against the hill Lucre, to wit, to the pillar of salt, that stood also within view of Sodom and its stinking lake, they marveled, as did Christian before, that men of such knowledge and ripeness of wit as they were, should be so blinded as to turn aside here. Only they considered again, that nature is not affected with the harms that others have met with, especially if that thing upon which they look has an attracting virtue upon the foolish eye.

I saw now, that they went on till they came to the river that was on this side of the Delectable Mountains; to the river where the fine trees grow on both sides, and whose leaves, if taken inwardly, are good against surfeits; where the meadows are green all the year long, and where they might lie down safely. (Ps. 23:2).

By this river-side, in the meadows, there were cotes and folds for sheep, a house built for the nourishing and bringing up of those lambs, the babes of those women that go on pilgrimage. Also there was here one that was entrusted with them, who could have compassion; and that could gather these lambs with his arm, and carry them in his bosom, and gently lead those that were with young. (Heb. 5:2; Isa. 40:11). Now, to the care of this man Christiana admonished her four daughters to commit their little ones, that by these waters they might be housed, harbored, succored, and nourished, and that none of them might be lacking in time to come. This man, if any of them go astray, or be lost, will bring them again; he will also bind up that which was broken, and will strengthen them that are sick. (Jer. 23:4; Ezek. 34:11-16). Here they will never want meat, drink, and clothing; here they will be kept from thieves and robbers; for this man will die before one of those committed to his trust shall be lost. Besides, here they shall be sure to have good nurture and admonition, and shall be taught to walk in right paths, and that you know is a favor of no small account. Also here, as you see, are delicate waters, pleasant meadows, dainty flowers, variety of trees, and such as bear wholesome fruit: fruit, not like that which Matthew ate of, that fell over the wall out of Beelzebub's garden; but fruit that procureth health where there is none, and that continueth and increaseth it where it is. So they were content to commit their little ones to him; and that which was also an encouragement to them so to do, was, for that all this was to be at the charge of the King, and so was as an hospital to young children and orphans.

Now they went on. And when they were come to By-path Meadow, to the stile over which Christian went with his fellow Hopeful, when they were taken by Giant Despair and put into Doubting Castle, they sat down, and consulted what was best to be done: to wit, now they were so strong, and had got such a man as Mr. Great-Heart for their conductor, whether they had not best to make an attempt upon the giant, demolish his castle, and if there were any pilgrims in it, to set them at liberty before they went any further. So one said one thing, and another said the contrary. One questioned if it was lawful to go upon unconsecrated ground; another said they might, provided their end was good; but Mr. Great-Heart said, Though that assertion offered last cannot be universally true, yet I have a commandment to resist sin, to overcome evil, to fight the good fight of faith: and I pray, with whom should I fight this good fight, if not with Giant Despair? I will therefore attempt the taking away of his life, and the demolishing of Doubting Castle. Then said he, Who will go with me? Then said old Honest, I will. And so will we too, said Christiana's four sons, Matthew, Samuel,

Joseph, and James; for they were young men and strong. (1 John 2:13,14). So they left the women in the road, and with them Mr. Feeble-mind, and Mr. Ready-to-halt with his crutches, to be their guard until they came back; for in that place the Giant Despair dwelt so near, they keeping in the road, a little child might lead them. (Is. 11:6).

So Mr. Great-Heart, old Honest, and the four young men, went to go up to Doubting Castle, to look for Giant Despair. When they came at the castle gate, they knocked for entrance with an unusual noise. At that the old Giant comes to the gate, and Diffidence his wife follows. Then said he, Who and what is he that is so hardy, as after this manner to molest the Giant Despair? Mr. Great-Heart replied, It is I, Great-Heart, one of the King of the Celestial country's conductors of pilgrims to their place; and I demand of thee that thou open thy gates for my entrance: prepare thyself also to fight, for I am come to take away thy head; and to demolish Doubting Castle.

Now Giant Despair, because he was a giant, thought no man could overcome him: and again thought he, Since heretofore I have made a conquest of angels, shall Great-Heart make me afraid? So he harnessed himself, and went out. He had a cap of steel upon his head, a breast-plate of fire girded to him, and he came out in iron shoes, with a great club in his hand. Then these six men made up to him, and beset him behind and before: also, when Diffidence the giantess came up to help him, old Mr. Honest cut her down at one blow. Then they fought for their lives, and Giant Despair was brought down to the ground, but was very loth die. He struggled hard, and had, as they say, as many lives as a cat; but Great-Heart was his death, for he left him not till he had severed his head from his shoulders.

Then they fell to demolishing Doubting Castle, and that you know might with ease be done, since Giant Despair was dead. They were seven days in destroying of that; and in it of pilgrims they found one Mr. Despondency, almost starved to death, and one Much-afraid, his daughter: these two they saved alive. But it would have made you wonder to have seen the dead bodies that lay here and there in the castle yard, and how full of dead men's bones the dungeon was.

When Mr. Great-Heart and his companions had performed this exploit, they took Mr. Despondency, and his daughter Much-afraid, into their protection; for they were honest people, though they were prisoners in Doubting Castle to that tyrant Giant Despair. They, therefore, I say, took with them the head of the giant, (for his body they had buried under a heap of stones,) and down to the road and to their companions they came, and showed them what they had done. Now, when Feeble-mind and Ready-to-halt saw that it was the head of Giant Despair indeed, they were very jocund and merry. Now Christiana, if need was, could play upon the viol, and her daughter Mercy upon the lute: so, since they were so merry disposed, she played them a lesson, and Ready-to-halt would dance. So he took Despondency's daughter, Much-afraid, by the hand, and to dancing they went in the road. True, he could not dance without one crutch in his hand, but I promise you he footed it well: also the girl was to be commended, for she answered the music handsomely.

As for Mr. Despondency, the music was not so much to him; he was for feeding rather than dancing, for that he was almost starved. So Christiana gave him some of her bottle of spirits for present relief, and then prepared him something to eat; and in a little time the old gentleman came to himself, and began to be finely revived.

Now I saw in my dream, when all these things were finished, Mr. Great-Heart took the head of Giant Despair, and set it upon a pole by the highway-side, right over against the pillar that Christian erected for a caution to pilgrims that came after, to take heed of entering into his grounds.

Then he writ under it upon a marble stone these verses following:

"This is the head of him whose name only
In former times did pilgrims terrify.
His castle's down, and Diffidence his wife
Brave Mr. Great-Heart has bereft of life.
Despondency, his daughter Much-afraid,
Great-Heart for them also the man has play'd.
Who hereof doubts, if he'll but cast his eye
Up hither, may his scruples satisfy.
This head also, when doubting cripples dance,
Doth show from fears they have deliverance."

When these men had thus bravely showed themselves against Doubting Castle, and had slain Giant Despair, they went forward, and went on till they came to the Delectable Mountains, where Christian and Hopeful refreshed themselves with the varieties of the place. They also acquainted themselves with the shepherds there, who welcomed them, as they had done Christian before, unto the Delectable Mountains.

Now the shepherds seeing so great a train follow Mr. Great-Heart, (for with him they were well acquainted,) they said unto him, Good sir, you have got a goodly company here; pray where did you find all these?

Then Mr. Great-Heart replied,

"First, here is Christiana and her train,
Her sons, and her sons' wives, who, like the wain,
Keep by the pole, and do by compass steer
From sin to grace, else they had not been here.
Next here's old Honest come on pilgrimage,
Ready-to-halt too, who I dare engage
True-hearted is, and so is Feeble-mind,
Who willing was not to be left behind.
Despondency, good man, is coming after,
And so also is Much-afraid, his daughter.
May we have entertainment here, or must
We further go? Let's knew whereon to trust."

Then said the shepherds, This is a comfortable company. You are welcome to us; for we have for the feeble, as well as for the strong. Our Prince has an eye to what is done to the least of these; therefore Infirmity must not be a block to our entertainment. (Matt. 25:40). So they had them to the palace door, and then said unto them, Come in, Mr. Feeble-Mind; come in Mr. Ready-to-halt; Come in, Mr. Despondency, and Mrs. Much-afraid his daughter. These, Mr. Great-Heart, said the shepherds to the guide, we call in by name, for that they are most subject to draw back; but as for you, and the rest that are strong, we leave you to your wonted liberty. Then said Mr. Great-Heart, This day I see that grace doth shine in your faces, and that you are my Lord's shepherds indeed; for that you have not pushed these diseased neither with side nor shoulder, but have rather strewed their way into the palace with flowers, as you should. (Ez. 34:21).

So the feeble and weak went in, and Mr. Great-Heart and the rest did follow. When they were also set down, the shepherds said to those of the weaker sort, What is it that you would have? for, said they, all things must be managed here to the supporting of the weak, as well as to the warning of the unruly. So they made them a feast of things easy of digestion, and that were pleasant to the palate and nourishing; the which when they had received, they went to their rest, each one respectively unto his proper place.

When morning was come, because the mountains were high and the day clear, and because it was the custom of the shepherds to show the pilgrims before their departure some rarities, therefore, after they were ready, and had refreshed themselves, the shepherds took them out into the fields, and showed them first what they had shown to Christian before.

Then they had them to some new places. The first was Mount Marvel, where they looked, and beheld a man at a distance that tumbled the hills about with words. Then they asked the shepherds what that should mean. So they told them, that that man was the son of one Mr. Great-grace, of whom you read in the first part of the records of the Pilgrim's Progress; and he is set there to teach pilgrims how to believe down, or to tumble out of their ways, what difficulties they should meet with, by faith. (Mark 11:23,24). Then said Mr. Great-Heart, I know him; he is a man above many.

Then they had them to another place, called Mount Innocence. And there they saw a man clothed all in white; and two men,

Prejudice and Ill-will, continually casting dirt upon him. Now behold, the dirt, whatsoever they cast at him, would in a little time fall off again, and his garment would look as clear as if no dirt had been cast thereat. Then said the pilgrims, What means this? The shepherds answered, This man is named Godlyman, and this garment is to show the innocency of his life. Now, those that throw dirt at him are such as hate his well-doing; but, as you see the dirt will not stick upon his clothes, so it shall be with him that liveth innocently in the world. Whoever they be that would make such men dirty, they labor all in vain; for God, by that a little time is spent, will cause that their innocence shall break forth as the light, and their righteousness as the noonday.

Then they took them, and had them to Mount Charity, where they showed them a man that had a bundle of cloth lying before him, out of which he cut coats and garments for the poor that stood about him; yet his bundle or roll of cloth was never the less. Then said they, What should this be? This is, said the shepherds, to show you, that he who has a heart to give of his labor to the poor, shall never want wherewithal. He that watereth shall be watered himself. And the cake that the widow gave to the prophet did not cause that she had the less in her barrel.

They had them also to the place where they saw one Fool and one Want-wit washing an Ethiopian, with intention to make him white; but the more they washed him, the blacker he was. Then they asked the shepherds what that should mean. So they told them, saying, Thus it is with the vile person; all means used to get such a one a good name, shall in conclusion tend but to make him more abominable. Thus it was with the Pharisees; and so it shall be with all hypocrites.

Then said Mercy, the wife of Matthew, to Christiana her mother, Mother, I would, if it might be, see the hole in the hill, or that commonly called the By-way to hell. So her mother brake her mind to the shepherds. Then they went to the door; it was on the side of an hill; and they opened it, and bid Mercy hearken a while. So she hearkened, and heard one saying, Cursed be my father for holding of my feet back from the way of peace and life. Another said, Oh that I had been torn in pieces before I had, to save my life, lost my soul! And another said, If I were to live again, how would I deny myself, rather than to come to this place! Then there was as if the very earth groaned and quaked under the feet of this young woman for fear; so she looked white, and came trembling away, saying, Blessed be he and she that is delivered from this place!

Now, when the shepherds had shown them all these things, then they had them back to the palace, and entertained them with what the house would afford. But Mercy, being a young and married woman, longed for something that she saw there, but was ashamed to ask. Her mother-in-law then asked her what she ailed, for she looked as one not well. Then said Mercy, There is a looking-glass hangs up in the dining-room, off which I cannot take my mind; if, therefore, I have it not, I think I shall miscarry. Then said her mother, I will mention thy wants to the shepherds, and they will not deny thee. But she said, I am ashamed that these men should know that I longed. Nay, my daughter, said she, it is no shame, but a virtue, to long for such a thing as that. So Mercy said, Then mother, if you please, ask the shepherds if they are willing to sell it.

Now the glass was one of a thousand. It would present a man, one way, with his own features exactly; and turn it but another way, and it would show one the very face and similitude of the Prince of pilgrims himself. Yes, I have talked with them that can tell, and they have said that they have seen the very crown of thorns upon his head by looking in that glass; they have therein also seen the holes in his hands, his feet, and his side. Yea, such an excellency is there in this glass, that it will show him to one where they have a mind to see him, whether living or dead; whether in earth, or in heaven; whether in a state of humiliation, or in his exaltation; whether coming to suffer, or coming to reign. (James 1:23; 1 Cor. 13:12; 2 Cor. 3:18).

Christiana therefore went to the shepherds apart, (now the names of the shepherds were Knowledge, Experience, Watchful, and Sincere,) and said unto them, There is one of my daughters, a breeding woman, that I think doth long for something that she hath seen in this house; and she thinks that she shall miscarry if she should by you be denied.

Experience: Call her, call her, she shall assuredly have what we can help her to. So they called her, and said to her, Mercy, what is that thing thou wouldst have? Then she blushed, and said, The great glass that hangs up in the dining-room. So Sincere ran and fetched it, and with a joyful consent it was given her. Then she bowed her head, and gave thanks, and said, By this I know that I have obtained favor in your eyes.

They also gave to the other young women such things as they desired, and to their husbands great commendations, for that they had joined with Mr. Great-Heart in the slaying of Giant Despair, and the demolishing of Doubting Castle.

About Christiana's neck the shepherds put a bracelet, and so did they about the necks of her four daughters; also they put ear-rings in their ears, and jewels on their foreheads.

When they were minded to go hence, they let them go in peace, but gave not to them those certain cautions which before were given to Christian and his companion. The reason was, for that these had Great-Heart to be their guide, who was one that was well acquainted with things, and so could give them their cautions more seasonably, to wit, even when the danger was nigh the approaching. What cautions Christian and his companion had received of the shepherds, they had also lost by that the time was come that they had need to put them in practice. Wherefore, here was the advantage that this company had over the other.

From thence they went on singing, and they said,

"Behold how fitly are the stages set
For their relief that pilgrims are become,
And how they us receive without one let,
That make the other life our mark and home!

What novelties they have to us they give,
That we, though pilgrims, joyful lives may live;
They do upon us, too, such things bestow,
That show we pilgrims are, where'er we go."

THE EIGHTH STAGE

When they were gone from the shepherds, they quickly came to the place where Christian met with one Turn-away that dwelt in the town of Apostasy. Wherefore of him Mr. Great-Heart their guide now put them in mind, saying, This is the place where Christian met with one Turn-away, who carried with him the character of his rebellion at his back. And this I have to say concerning this man; he would hearken to no counsel, but once a falling, persuasion could not stop him. When he came to the place where the cross and sepulcher were, he did meet with one that did bid him look there; but he gnashed with his teeth, and stamped, and said he was resolved to go back to his own town. Before he came to the gate, he met with Evangelist, who offered to lay hands on him, to turn him into the way again; but this Turn-away resisted him, and having done much despite unto him, he got away over the wall, and so escaped his hand.

Then they went on; and just at the place where Little-Faith formerly was robbed, there stood a man with his sword drawn, and his face all over with blood. Then said Mr. Great-Heart, Who art thou? The man made answer, saying, I am one whose name is Valiant-for-truth. I am a pilgrim, and am going to the Celestial City. Now, as I was in my way, there were three men that did beset me, and propounded unto me these three things:

1. Whether I would become one of them.
2. Or go back from whence I came.
3. Or die upon the place. (Prov. 1:11-14).

To the first I answered, I had been a true man for a long season, and therefore it could not be expected that I should now cast in my lot with thieves. Then they demanded what I would say to the second. So I told them that the place from whence I came, had I not found incommodity there, I had not forsaken it at all; but finding it altogether unsuitable to me, and very unprofitable for me, I forsook it for this way. Then they asked me what I said to the third. And I told them my life cost far more dear than that I should lightly give it away. Besides, you have nothing to do thus to put things to my choice; wherefore at your peril be it if you meddle. Then these three, to wit, Wild-head, Inconsiderate, and Pragmatic, drew upon me, and I also drew upon them. So we fell to it, one against three, for the space of above three hours. They have left upon me, as you see, some of the marks of their valor, and have also carried away with them some of mine. They are but just now gone; I suppose they might, as the saying is, hear your horse dash, and so they betook themselves to flight.

Mr. Great-Heart: But here was great odds, three against one .

Valiant-for-Truth: 'Tis true; but little and more are nothing to him that has the truth on his side: "Though an host should encamp against me," said one, (Ps. 27:3), "my heart shall not fear: though war should rise against me, in this will I be confident," etc. Besides, said he, I have read in some records, that one man has fought an army: and how many did Samson slay with the jawbone of an ass!

Mr. Great-Heart: Then said the guide, Why did you not cry out, that some might have come in for your succor?

Valiant-for-Truth: So I did to my King, who I knew could hear me, and afford invisible help, and that was sufficient for me.

Mr. Great-Heart: Then said Great-Heart to Mr. Valiant-for-truth, Thou hast worthily behaved thyself; let me see thy sword. So he showed it him.

When he had taken it in his hand, and looked thereon awhile, he said, Ha, it is a right Jerusalem blade.

Valiant-for-Truth: It is so. Let a man have one of these blades, with a hand to wield it, and skill to use it, and he may venture upon an angel with it. He need not fear its holding, if he can but tell how to lay on. Its edge will never blunt. It will cut flesh and bones, and soul, and spirit, and all. (Heb. 4:12).

Mr. Great-Heart: But you fought a great while; I wonder you was not weary.

Valiant-for-Truth: I fought till my sword did cleave to my hand; and then they were joined together as if a sword grew out of my arm; and when the blood ran through my fingers, then I fought with most courage.

Mr. Great-Heart: Thou hast done well; thou hast resisted unto blood, striving against sin. Thou shalt abide by us, come in and go out with us; for we are thy companions. Then they took him and washed his wounds, and gave him of what they had, to refresh him: and so they went together.

Now, as they went on, because Mr. Great-Heart was delighted in him, (for he loved one greatly that he found to be a man of his hands,) and because there were in company those that were feeble and weak, therefore he questioned with him about many things; as first, what countryman he was.

Valiant-for-Truth: I am of Dark-land; for there was I born, and there my father and mother are still.

Mr. Great-Heart: Dark-land! said the guide; doth not that lie on the same coast with the City of Destruction?

Valiant-for-Truth: Yes, it doth. Now that which caused me to come on pilgrimage was this. We had one Mr. Tell-true come into our parts, and he told it about what Christian had done, that went from the City of Destruction; namely, how he had forsaken his wife and children, and had betaken himself to a pilgrim's life. It was also confidently reported, how he had killed a serpent that did come out to resist him in his journey; and how he got through to whither he intended. It was also told what welcome he had at all his Lord's lodgings, especially when he came to the gates of the Celestial City; for there, said the man, he was received with sound of trumpet by a company of shining ones. He told also how all the bells in the city did ring for joy at his reception, and what golden garments he was clothed with; with many other things that now I shall forbear to relate. In a word, that man so told the story of Christian and his travels that my heart fell into a burning haste to be gone after him; nor could father or mother stay me. So I got from them, and am come thus far on my way.

Mr. Great-Heart: You came in at the gate, did you not?

Valiant-for-Truth: Yes, yes; for the same man also told us, that all would be nothing if we did not begin to enter this way at the gate.

Mr. Great-Heart: Look you, said the guide to Christiana, the pilgrimage of your husband, and what he has gotten thereby, is spread abroad far and near.

Valiant-for-Truth: Why, is this Christian's wife?

Mr. Great-Heart: Yes, that it is; and these also are his four sons.

Valiant-for-Truth: What, and going on pilgrimage too?

Mr. Great-Heart: Yes, verily, they are following after.

Valiant-for-Truth: It glads me at the heart. Good man, how joyful will he be when he shall see them that would not go with him, yet to enter after him in at the gates into the Celestial City.

Mr. Great-Heart: Without doubt it will be a comfort to him; for, next to the joy of seeing himself there, it will be a joy to meet there his wife and children.

Valiant-for-Truth: But now you are upon that, pray let me hear your opinion about it. Some make a question whether we shall know one another when we are there.

Mr. Great-Heart: Do you think they shall know themselves then, or that they shall rejoice to see themselves in that bliss? And if they think they shall know and do this, why not know others, and rejoice in their welfare also? Again, since relations are our second self, though that state will be dissolved there, yet why may it not be rationally concluded that we shall be more glad to see them there than to see they are wanting?

Valiant-for-Truth: Well, I perceive whereabouts you are as to this. Have you any more things to ask me about my beginning to come on pilgrimage?

Mr. Great-Heart: Yes; were your father and mother willing that you should become a pilgrim?

Valiant-for-Truth: O no; they used all means imaginable to persuade me to stay at home.

Mr. Great-Heart: Why, what could they say against it?

Valiant-for-Truth: They said it was an idle life; and if I myself were not inclined to sloth and laziness, I would never countenance a pilgrim's condition.

Mr. Great-Heart: And what did they say else?

Valiant-for-Truth: Why, they told me that it was a dangerous way; yea, the most dangerous way in the world, said they, is that which the pilgrims go.

Mr. Great-Heart: Did they show you wherein this way is so dangerous?

Valiant-for-Truth: Yes; and that in many particulars.

Mr. Great-Heart: Name some of them.

Valiant-for-Truth: They told me of the Slough of Despond, where Christian was well-nigh smothered. They told me, that there were archers standing ready in Beelzebub-castle to shoot them who should knock at the Wicket-gate for entrance. They told me also of the wood and dark mountains; of the hill Difficulty; of the lions; and also of the three giants, Bloody-man, Maul, and Slay-good. They said, moreover, that there was a foul fiend haunted the Valley of Humiliation; and that Christian was by him almost bereft of life. Besides, said they, you must go over the Valley of the Shadow of Death, where the hobgoblins are, where the light is darkness, where the way is full of snares, pits, traps, and gins. They told me also of Giant Despair, of Doubting Castle, and of the ruin that the pilgrims met with here. Further they said I must go over the Enchanted Ground, which was dangerous; And that after all this I should find a river, over which there was no bridge; and that that river did lie betwixt me and the Celestial country.

Mr. Great-Heart: And was this all?

Valiant-for-Truth: No. They also told me that this way was full of deceivers, and of persons that lay in wait there to turn good men out of the path.

Mr. Great-Heart: But how did they make that out?

Valiant-for-Truth: They told me that Mr. Worldly Wiseman did lie there in wait to deceive. They said also, that there were Formality and Hypocrisy continually on the road. They said also, that By-ends, Talkative, or Demas, would go near to gather me up; that the Flatterer would catch me in his net; or that, with green-headed Ignorance, I would presume to go on to the gate, from whence he was sent back to the hole that was in the side of the hill, and made to go the by-way to hell.

Mr. Great-Heart: I promise you this was enough to discourage you; but did they make an end here?

Valiant-for-Truth: No, stay. They told me also of many that had tried that way of old, and that had gone a great way therein, to see if they could find something of the glory there that so many had so much talked of from time to time, and how they came back again, and befooled themselves for setting a foot out of doors in that path, to the satisfaction of all the country. And they named several that did so, as Obstinate and Pliable, Mistrust and Timorous, Turn-away and old Atheist, with several more; who, they said, had some of them gone far to see what they could find, but not one of them had found so much advantage by going as amounted to the weight of a feather.

Mr. Great-Heart: Said they anything more to discourage you?

Valiant-for-Truth: Yes. They told me of one Mr. Fearing, who was a pilgrim, and how he found his way so solitary that he never had a comfortable hour therein; also, that Mr. Despondency had like to have been starved therein: yea, and also (which I had almost forgot) that Christian himself, about whom there has been such a noise, after all his adventures for a celestial crown, was certainly drowned in the Black River, and never went a foot further; however it was smothered up.

Mr. Great-Heart: And did none of these things discourage you?

Valiant-for-Truth: No; they seemed but as so many nothings to me.

Mr. Great-Heart: How came that about?

Valiant-for-Truth: Why, I still believed what Mr. Tell-true had said; and that carried me beyond them all.

Mr. Great-Heart: Then this was your victory, even your faith.

Valiant-for-Truth: It was so. I believed, and therefore came out, got into the way, fought all that set themselves against me, and, by believing, am come to this place.

"Who would true valor see,
Let him come hither;
One here will constant be,
Come wind, come weather
There's no discouragement
Shall make him once relent
His first avow'd intent
To be a pilgrim.

Whoso beset him round
With dismal stories,
Do but themselves confound;
His strength the more is.
No lion can him fright,
He'll with a giant fight,
But he will have a right
To be a pilgrim.

Hobgoblin nor foul fiend
Can daunt his spirit;
He knows he at the end
Shall life inherit.
Then fancies fly away,
He'll not fear what men say;
He'll labor night and day
To be a pilgrim.

By this time they were got to the Enchanted Ground, where the air naturally tended to make one drowsy. And that place was all grown over with briars and thorns, excepting here and there, where was an enchanted arbor, upon which if a man sits, or in which if a man sleeps, it is a question, some say, whether ever he shall rise or wake again in this world. Over this forest, therefore, they went, both one and another, and Mr. Great-Heart went before, for that he was the guide; and Mr. Valiant-for-truth came behind, being rear-guard, for fear lest peradventure some fiend, or dragon, or giant, or thief, should fall upon their rear, and so do mischief. They went on here, each man with his sword drawn in his hand; for they knew it was a dangerous place. Also they cheered up one another as well as they could. Feeble-mind, Mr. Great-Heart commanded should come up after him; and Mr. Despondency was under the eye of Mr. Valiant.

Now they had not gone far, but a great mist and darkness fell upon them all; so that they could scarce, for a great while, the one see the other. Wherefore they were forced, for some time, to feel one for another by words; for they walked not by sight. But any one must think, that here was but sorry going for the best of them all; but how much worse for the women and children, who both of feet and heart were but tender! Yet so it was, that through the encouraging words of him that led in the front, and of him that brought them up behind, they made a pretty good shift to wag along.

The way also here was very wearisome, through dirt and slabbiness. Nor was there, on all this ground, so much as one inn or victualling-house wherein to refresh the feebler sort. Here, therefore, was grunting, and puffing, and sighing, while one tumbleth over a bush, another sticks fast in the dirt, and the children, some of them, lost their shoes in the mire; while one cries out, I am down; and another, Ho, where are you? and a third, The bushes have got such fast hold on me, I think I cannot get away from them.

Then they came at an arbor, warm, and promising much refreshing to the pilgrims; for it was finely wrought above-head, beautified with greens, furnished with benches and settles. It also had in it a soft couch, whereon the weary might lean. This, you must think, all things considered, was tempting; for the pilgrims already began to be foiled with the badness of the way: but there was not one of them that made so much as a motion to stop there. Yea, for aught I could perceive, they continually gave so good heed to the advice of their guide, and he did so faithfully tell them of dangers, and of the nature of the dangers when they were at them, that usually, when they were nearest to them, they did most pluck up their spirits, and hearten one another to deny the flesh. This arbor was called The Slothful's Friend, and was made on purpose to allure, if it might be, some of the pilgrims there to take up their rest when weary.

I saw them in my dream, that they went on in this their solitary ground, till they came to a place at which a man is apt to lose his way. Now, though when it was light their guide could well enough tell how to miss those ways that led wrong, yet in the dark he was put to a stand. But he had in his pocket a map of all ways leading to or from the Celestial City; wherefore he struck a light (for he never goes without his tinder-box also), and takes a view of his book or map, which bids him to be careful in that place to turn to the right hand. And had he not been careful here to look in his map, they had all, in probability, been smothered in the mud; for just a little before them, and that at the end of the cleanest way too, was a pit, none knows how deep, full of nothing but mud, there made on purpose to destroy the pilgrims in.

Then thought I with myself, Who that goeth on pilgrimage but would have one of these maps about him, that he may look, when he is at a stand, which is the way he must take?

Then they went on in this Enchanted Ground till they came to where there was another arbor, and it was built by the highway-side. And in that arbor there lay two men, whose names were Heedless and Too-bold. These two went thus far on pilgrimage; but here, being wearied with their journey, they sat down to rest themselves, and so fell fast asleep. When the pilgrims saw them, they stood still, and shook their heads; for they knew that the sleepers were in a pitiful case. Then they consulted what to do, whether to go on and leave them in their sleep, or to step to them and try to awake them; so they concluded to go to them and awake them, that is, if they could; but with this caution, namely, to take heed that they themselves did not sit down nor embrace the offered benefit of that arbor.

So they went in, and spake to the men, and called each by his name, for the guide, it seems, did know them; but there was no voice nor answer. Then the guide did shake them, and do what he could to disturb them. Then said one of them, I will pay you when I take my money. At which the guide shook his head. I will fight so long as I can hold my sword in my hand, said the other. At that, one of the children laughed.

Then said Christiana, What is the meaning of this? The guide said, They talk in their sleep. If you strike them, beat them, or whatever else you do to them, they will answer you after this fashion; or, as one of them said in old time, when the waves of the sea did beat upon him, and he slept as one upon the mast of a ship, (Prov. 23:34,35), When I awake, I will seek it yet again. You know, when men talk in their sleep, they say anything; but their words are not governed either by faith or reason. There is an incoherency in their words now, as there was before betwixt their going on pilgrimage and sitting down here. This, then, is the mischief of it: when heedless ones go on pilgrimage, 'tis twenty to one but they are served thus. For this Enchanted Ground is one of the last refuges that the enemy to pilgrims has; wherefore it is, as you see, placed almost at the end of the way, and so it standeth against us with the more advantage. For when, thinks the enemy, will these fools be so desirous to sit down as when they are weary? and when so like to be weary as when almost at their journey's end? Therefore it is, I say, that the Enchanted Ground is placed so nigh to the land Beulah, and so near the end of their race. Wherefore let pilgrims look to themselves, lest it happen to them as it has done to these that, as you see, are fallen asleep, and none can awake them.

Then the pilgrims desired with trembling to go forward; only they prayed their guide to strike a light, that they might go the rest of their way by the help of the light of a lantern. So he struck a light, and they went by the help of that through the rest of this way, though the darkness was very great. (2 Pet. 1:19). But the children began to be sorely weary, and they cried out unto him that loveth pilgrims, to make their way more comfortable. So by that they had gone a little further, a wind arose that drove away the fog, so the air became more clear. Yet they were not off (by much) of the Enchanted Ground; only now they could see one another better, and the way wherein they should walk.

Now when they were almost at the end of this ground, they perceived that a little before them was a solemn noise, as of one that was much concerned. So they went on and looked before them: and behold they saw, as they thought, a man upon his knees, with hands and eyes lifted up, and speaking, as they thought, earnestly to one that was above. They drew nigh, but could not tell what he said; so they went softly till he had done. When he had done, he got up, and began to run towards the Celestial City. Then Mr. Great-Heart called after him, saying, Soho, friend, let us have your company, if you go, as I suppose you do, to the Celestial City. So the man stopped, and they came up to him. But as soon as Mr. Honest saw him, he said, I know this man. Then said Mr. Valiant-for-truth, Prithee, who is it? It is one, said he, that comes from whereabout I dwelt. His name is Standfast; he is certainly a right good pilgrim.

So they came up to one another; and presently Standfast said to old Honest, Ho, father Honest, are you there? Aye, said he, that I am, as sure as you are there. Right glad am I, said Mr. Standfast, that I have found you on this road. And as glad am I, said the other, that I espied you on your knees. Then Mr. Standfast blushed, and said, But why, did you see me? Yes, that I did, quoth the other, and with my heart was glad at the sight. Why, what did you think? said Standfast. Think! said old Honest; what could I think? I thought we had an honest man upon the road, and therefore should have his company by and by. If you thought not amiss, said Standfast, how happy am I! But if I be not as I should, t is I alone must bear it. That is true, said the other; but your fear doth further confirm me that things are right betwixt the Prince of pilgrims and your soul. For he saith, "Blessed is the man that feareth always." (Prov. 28:14).

Valiant-for-Truth: Well but, brother, I pray thee tell us what was it that was the cause of thy being upon thy knees even now: was it for that some special mercy laid obligations upon thee, or how?

Standfast: Why, we are, as you see, upon the Enchanted Ground; and as I was coming along, I was musing with myself of what a dangerous nature the road in this place was, and how many that had come even thus far on pilgrimage, had here been stopped and been destroyed. I thought also of the manner of the death with which this place destroyeth men. Those that die here, die of no violent distemper: the death which such die is not grievous to them. For he that goeth away in a sleep, begins that journey with desire and pleasure. Yea, such acquiesce in the will of that disease.

Mr. Honest: Then Mr. Honest interrupting him, said, Did you see the two men asleep in the arbor?

Standfast: Aye, aye, I saw Heedless and Too-bold there; and for ought I know, there they will lie till they rot. (Prov. 10:7). But let me go on with my tale. As I was thus musing, as I said, there was one in very pleasant attire, but old, who presented herself to me, and offered me three things, to wit, her body, her purse, and her bed. Now the truth is, I was both weary and sleepy. I am also as poor as an owlet, and that perhaps the witch knew. Well, I repulsed her once and again, but she put by my repulses, and smiled. Then I began to be angry; but she mattered that nothing at all. Then she made offers again, and said, if I would be ruled by her, she would make me great and happy; for, said she, I am the mistress of the world, and men are made happy by me. Then I asked her name, and she told me it was Madam Bubble. This set me further from her; but she still followed me with enticements. Then I betook me, as you saw, to my knees, and with hands lifted up, and cries, I prayed to Him that had said he would help. So, just as you came up, the gentlewoman went her way. Then I continued to give thanks for this my great deliverance; for I verily believe she intended no good, but rather sought to make stop of me in my journey.

Mr. Honest: Without doubt her designs were bad. But stay, now you talk of her, methinks I either have seen her, or have read some story of her.

Standfast: Perhaps you have done both.

Mr. Honest: Madam Bubble! Is she not a tall, comely dame, something of a swarthy complexion?

Standfast: Right, you hit it: she is just such a one.

Mr. Honest: Doth she not speak very smoothly, and give you a smile at the end of a sentence?

Standfast: You fall right upon it again, for these are her very actions.

Mr. Honest: Doth she not wear a great purse by her side, and is not her hand often in it, fingering her money, as if that was her heart's delight.

Standfast: 'Tis just so; had she stood by all this while, you could not more amply have set her forth before me, nor have better described her features.

Mr. Honest: Then he that drew her picture was a good limner, and he that wrote of her said true.

Mr. Great-Heart: This woman is a witch, and it is by virtue of her sorceries that this ground is enchanted. Whoever doth lay his head down in her lap, had as good lay it down on that block over which the axe doth hang; and whoever lay their eyes upon her beauty are counted the enemies of God. This is she that maintaineth in their splendor all those that are the enemies of pilgrims. (James 4:4). Yea, this is she that has bought off many a man from a pilgrim's life. She is a great gossiper; she is always, both she and her daughters, at one pilgrim's heels or another, now commending, and then preferring the excellences of this life. She is a bold and impudent slut: she will talk with any man. She always laugheth poor pilgrims to scorn, but highly commends the rich. If there be one cunning to get money in a place, she will speak well of him from house to house. She loveth banqueting and feasting mainly well; she is always at one full table or another. She has given it out in some places that she is a goddess, and therefore some do worship her. She has her time, and open places of cheating; and she will say and avow it, that none can show a good comparable to hers. She promiseth to dwell with children's children, if they will but love her and make much of her. She will cast out of her purse gold like dust in some places and to some persons. She loves to be sought after, spoken well of, and to lie in the bosoms of men. She is never weary of commending her commodities, and she loves them most that think best of her. She will promise to some crowns and kingdoms, if they will but take her advice; yet many has she brought to the halter, and ten thousand times more to hell.

Standfast: Oh, said Standfast, what a mercy is it that I did resist her; for whither might she have drawn me!

Mr. Great-Heart: Whither? nay, none but God knows whither. But in general, to be sure, she would have drawn thee into many foolish and hurtful lusts, which drown men in destruction and perdition. (1 Tim. 6:9). 'Twas she that set Absalom against his father, and Jeroboam against his master. T was she that persuaded Judas to sell his Lord; and that prevailed with Demas to forsake the godly pilgrim's life. None can tell of the mischief that she doth. She makes variance betwixt rulers and subjects, betwixt parents and children, betwixt neighbor and neighbor, betwixt a man and his wife, betwixt a man and himself, betwixt the flesh and the spirit. Wherefore, good Mr. Standfast, be as your name is, and when you have done all, stand.

At this discourse there was among the pilgrims a mixture of joy and trembling; but at length they broke out and sang,

"What danger is the Pilgrim in!
How many are his foes!
How many ways there are to sin
No living mortal knows.

Some in the ditch are spoiled, yea, can
Lie tumbling in the mire:
Some, though they shun the frying-pan
Do leap into the fire."

After this, I beheld until they were come into the land of Beulah, where the sun shineth night and day. Here, because they were weary, they betook themselves a while to rest. And because this country was common for pilgrims, and because the orchards and vineyards that were here belonged to the King of the Celestial country, therefore they were licensed to make bold with any of his things. But a little while soon refreshed them here; for the bells did so ring, and the trumpets continually sound so melodiously, that they could not sleep, and yet they received as much refreshing as if they had slept their sleep ever so soundly. Here also all the noise of them that walked the streets was, More pilgrims are come to town! And another would answer, saying, And so many went over the water, and were let in at the golden gates to-day! They would cry again, There is now a legion of shining ones just come to town, by which we know that there are more pilgrims upon the road; for here they come to wait for them, and to comfort them after all their sorrow. Then the pilgrims got up, and walked to and fro. But how were their ears now filled with heavenly noises, and their eyes delighted with celestial visions! In this land they heard nothing, saw nothing, felt nothing, smelt nothing, tasted nothing that was offensive to their stomach or mind; only when they tasted of the water of the river over which they were to go, they thought that it tasted a little bitterish to the palate; but it proved sweeter when it was down.

In this place there was a record kept of the names of them that had been pilgrims of old, and a history of all the famous acts that they had done. It was here also much discoursed, how the river to some had had its flowings, and what ebbings it has had while others have gone over. It has been in a manner dry for some, while it has overflowed its banks for others.

In this place the children of the town would go into the King's gardens, and gather nosegays for the pilgrims, and bring them to them with much affection. Here also grew camphor, with spikenard and saffron, calamus and cinnamon, with all the trees of frankincense, myrrh, and aloes, with all chief spices. With these the pilgrims' chambers were perfumed while they stayed here; and with these were their bodies anointed, to prepare them to go over the river, when the time appointed was come.

Now, while they lay here, and waited for the good hour, there was a noise in the town that there was a post come from the Celestial City, with matter of great importance to one Christiana, the wife of Christian the pilgrim. So inquiry was made for her, and the house was found out where she was. So the post presented her with a letter. The contents were, Hail, good woman; I bring thee tidings that the Master calleth for thee, and expecteth that thou shouldst stand in his presence in clothes of immortality within these ten days.

When he had read this letter to her, he gave her therewith a sure token that he was a true messenger, and was come to bid her make haste to be gone. The token was, an arrow with a point sharpened with love, let easily into her heart, which by degrees wrought so effectually with her, that at the time appointed she must be gone.

When Christiana saw that her time was come, and that she was the first of this company that was to go over, she called for Mr. Great-Heart her guide, and told him how matters were. So he told her he was heartily glad of the news, and could have been glad had the post come for him. Then she bid him that he should give advice how all things should be prepared for her journey. So he told her, saying, Thus and thus it must be, and we that survive will accompany you to the river-side.

Then she called for her children, and gave them her blessing, and told them that she had read with comfort the mark that was set in their foreheads, and was glad to see them with her there, and that they had kept their garments so white. Lastly, she bequeathed to the poor that little she had, and commanded her sons and daughters to be ready against the messenger should come for them.

When she had spoken these words to her guide, and to her children, she called for Mr. Valiant-for-truth, and said unto him, Sir, you have in all places showed yourself true-hearted; be faithful unto death, and my King will give you a crown of life. (Rev. 2:10). I would also entreat you to have an eye to my children; and if at any time you see them faint, speak comfortably to them. For my daughters, my sons' wives, they have been faithful, and a fulfilling of the promise upon them will be their end. But she gave Mr. Standfast a ring.

Then she called for old Mr. Honest, and said of him, "Behold an Israelite indeed, in whom is no guile!" (John 1:47). Then said he, I wish you a fair day when you set out for Mount Zion, and shall be glad to see that you go over the river dry-shod. But she answered, Come wet, come dry, I long to be gone; for however the weather is in my journey, I shall have time enough when I come there to sit down and rest me and dry me.

Then came in that good man Mr. Ready-to-halt, to see her. So she said to him, Thy travel hitherto has been with difficulty; but that will make thy rest the sweeter. Watch, and be ready; for at an hour when you think not, the messenger may come.

After him came Mr. Despondency and his daughter Much-afraid, to whom she said, You ought, with thankfulness, forever to remember your deliverance from the hands of Giant Despair, and out of Doubting Castle. The effect of that mercy is, that you are brought with safety hither. Be ye watchful, and cast away fear; be sober, and hope to the end.

Then she said to Mr. Feeble-mind, Thou wast delivered from the mouth of Giant Slay-good, that thou mightest live in the light of the living, and see thy King with comfort. Only I advise thee to repent of thine aptness to fear and doubt of his goodness, before he sends for thee; lest thou shouldst, when he comes, be forced to stand before him for that fault with blushing.

Now the day drew on that Christiana must be gone. So the road was full of people to see her take her journey. But behold, all the banks beyond the river were full of horses and chariots, which were come down from above to accompany her to the city gate. So she came forth, and entered the river, with a beckon of farewell to those that followed her. The last words that she was heard to say were, I come, Lord, to be with thee and bless thee! So her children and friends returned to their place, for those that waited for Christiana had carried her out of their sight. So she went and called, and entered in at the gate with all the ceremonies of joy that her husband Christian had entered with before her. At her departure, the children wept. But Mr. Great-Heart and Mr. Valiant played upon the well tuned cymbal and harp for joy. So all departed to their respective places.

In process of time there came a post to the town again, and his business was with Mr. Ready-to-halt. So he inquired him out, and said, I am come from Him whom thou hast loved and followed, though upon crutches; and my message is to tell thee, that he expects thee at his table to sup with him in his kingdom, the next day after Easter; wherefore prepare thyself for this journey. Then he also gave him a token that he was a true messenger, saying, "I have broken thy golden bowl, and loosed thy silver cord." (Eccl. 12:6).

After this, Mr. Ready-to-halt called for his fellow-pilgrims, and told them, saying, I am sent for, and God shall surely visit you also. So he desired Mr. Valiant to make his will. And because he had nothing to bequeath to them that should survive him but his crutches, and his good wishes, therefore thus he said, These crutches I bequeath to my son that shall tread in my steps, with a hundred warm wishes that he may prove better than I have been.

Then he thanked Mr. Great-Heart for his conduct and kindness, and so addressed himself to his journey. When he came to the brink of the river, he said, Now I shall have no more need of these crutches, since yonder are chariots and horses for me to ride on. The last words he was heard to say were, Welcome life! So he went his way.

After this, Mr. Feeble-mind had tidings brought him that the post sounded his horn at his chamber door. Then he came in, and told him, saying, I am come to tell thee that thy Master hath need of thee, and that in a very little time thou must behold his face in brightness. And take this as a token of the truth of my message: "Those that look out at the windows shall be darkened." (Eccl. 12:3). Then Mr. Feeble-mind called for his friends, and told them what errand had been brought unto him, and what token he had received of the truth of the message. Then he said, since I have nothing to bequeath to any, to what purpose should I make a will? As for my feeble mind, that I will leave behind me, for that I shall have no need of it in the place whither I go, nor is it worth bestowing upon the poorest pilgrims: wherefore, when I am gone, I desire that you, Mr. Valiant, would bury it in a dunghill. This done, and the day being come on which he was to depart, he entered the river as the rest. His last words were, Hold out, faith and patience! So he went over to the other side.

When days had many of them passed away, Mr. Despondency was sent for; for a post was come, and brought this message to him: Trembling man! these are to summon thee to be ready with the King by the next Lord's day, to shout for joy for thy deliverance from all thy doubtings. And, said the messenger, that my message is true, take this for a proof: so he gave him a grasshopper to be a burden unto him. (Eccl. 12:5).

Now Mr. Despondency's daughter, whose name was Much-afraid, said, when she heard what was done, that she would go with her father. Then Mr. Despondency said to his friends, Myself and my daughter, you know what we have been, and how troublesomely we have behaved ourselves in every company. My will and my daughter's is, that our desponds and slavish fears be by no man ever received, from the day of our departure, forever; for I know that after my death they will offer themselves to others. For, to be plain with you, they are ghosts which we entertained when we first began to be pilgrims, and could never shake them off after; and they will walk about, and seek entertainment of the pilgrims: but for our sakes, shut the doors upon them. When the time was come for them to depart, they went up to the brink of the river. The last words of Mr. Despondency were, Farewell, night; welcome, day! His daughter went through the river singing, but none could understand what she said.

Then it came to pass a while after, that there was a post in the town that inquired for Mr. Honest. So he came to the house where he was, and delivered to his hand these lines: Thou art commanded to be ready against this day seven-night, to present thyself before thy Lord at his Father's house. And for a token that my message is true, "All the daughters of music shall be brought low." (Eccl. 12:4). Then Mr. Honest called for his friends, and said unto them, I die, but shall make no will. As for my honesty, it shall go with me; let him that comes after be told of this. When the day that he was to be gone was come, he addressed himself to go over the river. Now the river at that time over-flowed its banks in some places; but Mr. Honest, in his lifetime, had spoken to one Good-conscience to meet him there, the which he also did, and lent him his hand, and so helped him over. The last words of Mr. Honest were, Grace reigns! So he left the world.

After this it was noised abroad that Mr. Valiant-for-truth was taken with a summons by the same post as the other, and had this for a token that the summons was true, "That his pitcher was broken at the fountain." (Eccl. 12:6). When he understood it, he called for his friends, and told them of it. Then said he, I am going to my Father's; and though with great difficulty I have got hither, yet now I do not repent me of all the trouble I have been at to arrive where I am. My sword I give to him that shall succeed me in my pilgrimage, and my courage and skill to him that can get it. My marks and scars I carry with me, to be a witness for me that I have fought His battles who will now be my rewarder. When the day that he must go hence was come, many accompanied him to the river-side, into which as he went, he said, "Death, where is thy sting?" And as he went down deeper, he said, "Grave, where is thy victory?" (1 Cor. 15:55). So he passed over, and all the trumpets sounded for him on the other side.

Then there came forth a summons for Mr. Standfast. This Mr. Standfast was he whom the rest of the pilgrims found upon his knees in the Enchanted Ground. And the post brought it him open in his hands: the contents thereof were, that he must prepare for a change of life, for his Master was not willing that he should be so far from him any longer. At this Mr. Standfast was put into a muse. Nay, said the messenger, you need not doubt of the truth of my message; for here is a token of the truth thereof, "Thy wheel is broken at the cistern." Eccl. 12:6. Then he called to him Mr. Great-Heart, who was their guide, and said unto him, Sir, although it was not my hap to be much in your good company during the days of my pilgrimage, yet, since the time I knew you, you have been profitable to me. When I came from home, I left behind me a wife and five small children; let me entreat you, at your return, (for I know that you go and return to your Master's house, in hopes that you may yet be a conductor to more of the holy pilgrims,) that you send to my family, and let them be acquainted with all that hath and shall happen unto me. Tell them moreover of my happy arrival at this place, and of the present and late blessed condition

I am in. Tell them also of Christian and Christiana his wife, and how she and her children came after her husband. Tell them also of what a happy end she made, and whither she is gone. I have little or nothing to send to my family, unless it be prayers and tears for them; of which it will suffice that you acquaint them, if peradventure they may prevail. When Mr. Standfast had thus set things in order, and the time being come for him to haste him away, he also went down to the river. Now there was a great calm at that time in the river; wherefore Mr. Standfast, when he was about half-way in, stood a while, and talked with his companions that had waited upon him thither. And he said, This river has been a terror to many; yea, the thoughts of it also have often frightened me; but now methinks I stand easy; my foot is fixed upon that on which the feet of the priests that bare the ark of the covenant stood while Israel went over Jordan. (Josh. 3:17). The waters indeed are to the palate bitter, and to the stomach cold; yet the thoughts of what I am going to, and of the convoy that waits for me on the other side, do lie as a glowing coal at my heart. I see myself now at the end of my journey; my toilsome days are ended. I am going to see that head which was crowned with thorns, and that face which was spit upon for me. I have formerly lived by hearsay and faith; but now I go where I shall live by sight, and shall be with him in whose company I delight myself. I have loved to hear my Lord spoken of; and wherever I have seen the print of his shoe in the earth, there I have coveted to set my foot too. His name has been to me as a civet-box; yea, sweeter than all perfumes. His voice to me has been most sweet, and his countenance I have more desired than they that have most desired the light of the sun. His words I did use to gather for my food, and for antidotes against my faintings. He hath held me, and hath kept me from mine iniquities; yea, my steps hath he strengthened in his way.

Now, while he was thus in discourse, his countenance changed; his strong man bowed under him: and after he had said, Take me, for I come unto thee, he ceased to be seen of them.

But glorious it was to see how the open region was filled with horses and chariots, with trumpeters and pipers, with singers and players upon stringed instruments, to welcome the pilgrims as they went up, and followed one another in at the beautiful gate of the city.

As for Christiana's children, the four boys that Christiana brought, with their wives and children, I did not stay where I was till they were gone over. Also, since I came away, I heard one say that they were yet alive, and so would be for the increase of the church, in that place where they were, for a time.

Should it be my lot to go that way again, I may give those that desire it an account of what I here am silent about: meantime I bid my reader:

Farwell, The End

LUMEN™

Other titles available *from* Lumen Classics

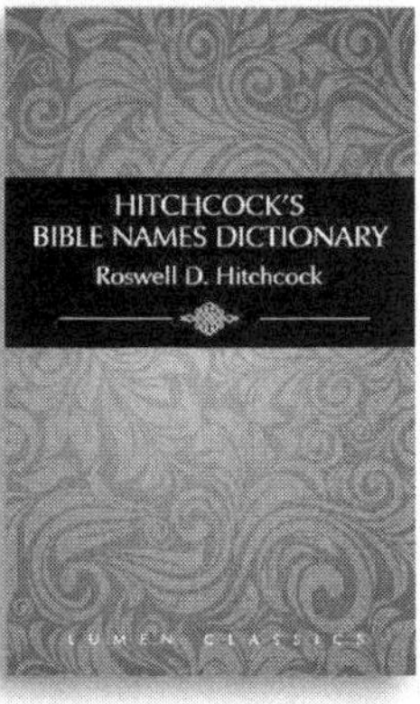

ISBN: 978-0-9835608-9-0

ISBN: 978-0-9835608-5-2

ISBN: 978-0-9835608-6-9

ISBN: 978-1-939900-03-6

ISBN: 978-0-9835608-8-3

ISBN: 978-1-939900-01-2

ISBN: 978-0-9835608-7-6

For a complete list of
LUMEN Christian Products
visit *www.stl-distribution.com/ lumen*